Strange Lake Adventure

Sharon Siamon

cover and illustrations
by David Simpson

gage EDUCATIONAL PUBLISHING COMPANY
A DIVISION OF CANADA PUBLISHING CORPORATION
TORONTO ONTARIO CANADA

ISBN 0-7715-5982-8

13 14 15 WC 95 94

Contents

Where the adventure took place

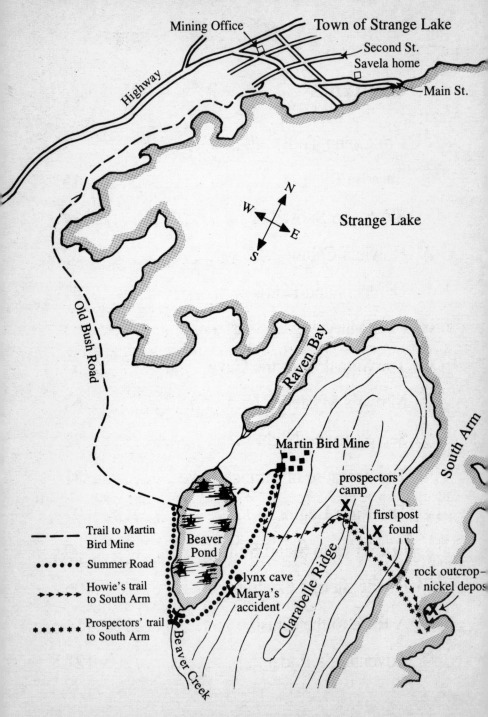

Town of Strange Lake

Mining Office

Second St.
Savela home

Highway

Main St.

Strange Lake

N
W   E
S

Old Bush Road

Raven Bay

South Arm

Martin Bird Mine

prospectors' camp

first post found

Beaver Pond

lynx cave
Marya's accident

Clarabelle Ridge

rock outcrop– nickel depos

Trail to Martin Bird Mine

Summer Road

Howie's trail to South Arm

Prospectors' trail to South Arm

Beaver Creek

1

I'm Going Too!

It was a frosty Friday morning in February —
and a school holiday!

Anna Savela was stretched out on the living-
room rug, trying to read her book on dinosaurs.
Her ten-year-old brother Eric was pretending that
the big armchair was his snowmobile. As usual,
he was making so much noise that Anna could
hardly think.

Suddenly, their older sister Marya burst into
the room. "Hey, kids!" she cried. "Guess what!"

Marya was wearing her bright blue snowmobile suit. Her cheeks were red from the cold —
and from excitement.

Anna and Eric could tell from the look on
Marya's face that she was excited about something
really special.

"What is it? Don't make us guess; just tell
us!" Eric shouted, turning a somersault out of his
chair.

5

"I'm going to take Howie Stern's supplies
out to him!" Marya cried. "Dad can't go because
of his sore leg, and Mom's still in Timmins.
Somebody has to go, because Howie Stern needs
his food and medicine. So...Dad's going to let
me go. Isn't it terrific? Get your suit on, Eric.
You're coming too!"

Eric and Anna both leaped to their feet. This
was exciting!

Howie Stern was an old prospector. He lived
all alone, with his cat Toby, at an old mine far in
the bush. For two years the children's father had
been taking his supplies in by snowmobile when
winter snow blocked the bush road.

"Oh, boy!" cried Eric. "Is Dad really going to let us take his new snowmobile out to the Martin Bird mine?"

"Yes, but he's still worried about it. So hurry and get ready. Dad wants us to get out there before noon."

Sixteen-year-old Marya turned and raced for the back door. Eric and Anna were right on her heels.

As Marya disappeared out the door, they could hear a loud "var-oom, var-oom." Their father was warming up the engine of his powerful, new snowmobile.

Eric grabbed his snowmobile suit and stuffed in one leg. At the same time he reached wildly for sweaters, scarves, and mitts. "Got to dress warmly," he muttered. "It'll be freezing cold. Where's my boot?"

Anna was dressing quickly too — but without all the fuss that Eric made. People often called her the "quiet one," but that was because they usually saw her beside Eric. "He's more like a hurricane than a human being!" she thought, as she watched her brother hopping about and waving his arms.

"Why are you putting on *your* snowmobile suit?" Eric asked. "You're not going anywhere. Did you see my boot?"

Anna was bending over, zipping up her leg zippers and thinking fast. She couldn't let Eric and Marya go off on this wonderful adventure without her!

All her life Anna had heard stories about Howie Stern, the prospector, but she had never seen him. Now she might be able to meet him — in his own cabin!

Anna wanted to ride down the white trail between the pine trees that led to the old Martin Bird mine. She wanted to see Howie's log cabin with the smoke coming out of the chimney. She might even see a moose on the way...or a deer! "I just *have* to go with them," Anna thought.

Just then the door opened, and Marya's dark, curly head appeared. "Hurry up, Eric. I need you out here," she said.

"I can't find my stupid *boot*!" howled Eric. "Somebody's taken it!" But Marya had closed the door again.

"You probably threw it in that heap over there," said Anna, pointing to a big pile of boots in the corner.

Eric dropped to his knees and started heaving boots in all directions.

Anna zipped up her snowmobile suit and ran out the door. She was ready. Maybe Eric wouldn't find his boot. Then Marya would take *her* instead.

Anna blinked as the bright winter sun hit her eyes. There was a big can of lard on the porch, and she carried it over to where Marya was stuffing supplies into packsacks.

"Marya," Anna said, "could I come?"

"Where's Eric?" Marya asked.

"Still getting dressed," said Anna. "Could I, Marya?"

Marya stood up. "I know you want to come, Anna," she said, seriously. "But it's ten kilometres out and ten back — and the temperature is minus thirteen." She squinted up at the blue sky. "The weather looks great now, but Dad says it might snow later. We'd have to stay overnight if there's a storm. It could be pretty cold and uncomfortable."

Anna's heart sank to the toes of her snowmobile boots. How wonderful to have to stay at Howie Stern's cabin overnight! Nothing in her life could ever make up for missing that.

"I don't get cold," she said bravely. "I'm not afraid."

Marya put down the pack that she was filling and put her arm around Anna's shoulders. She

9

could see the hope in Anna's blue eyes. Marya was sixteen, but she could remember what it was like to be nine and too young for everything.

"Anna," she said, "listen. There's only room for two on the snowmobile. We might get stuck in the deep snow in the bush. I'd need Eric to help me lift the back end of the machine if that happened. Could you do that?"

Anna shook her head. Looking at the big orange snowmobile, with its heavy load of supplies, she knew that she could never lift it out of a snowbank. She was just too small.

"I'm sorry," Marya said. "Maybe next time. If you want to help, though, you could bring out the snowshoes. Dad says we'll need them once we're at the cabin."

"You certainly will," Mr. Savela said, lifting his head from under the hood of the snowmobile. "Never go into the bush this time of year without snowshoes."

Anna turned and went back up the porch steps. She opened the back door — and ducked. A big, black snowmobile boot zinged past her ear and thumped into the wall. Eric was still looking for his boot. Anna dodged past him to get the snowshoes off a peg.

"You took my boot and hid it so I couldn't go. You hid it! Where did you hide it?" Eric called angrily. His face was red. He was hot in his snowmobile suit, and cross.

"Don't be silly. I didn't hide your boot," Anna said.

"Well, help me find it then," Eric shouted.

"Can't," said Anna. "I have to take these snowshoes out to Marya."

Anna went back outside and handed the two pairs of snowshoes to Marya. Mr. Savela was leaning on his cane and looking at the loaded snowmobile with a frown. "You'll be back-heavy with Eric on there, and the packs," he said slowly.

Anna felt a shiver of hope. Eric was *too* heavy. Maybe they'd have to take her because she was lighter!

"I guess you'll have to take the sled for the supplies," her father said.

Anna's hope disappeared like a melted icicle.

"I'll get the sled," she called, running to the garage where it was stored. She didn't want her father and Marya to see how disappointed she was.

When Anna came back with the shiny silver sled, Marya bent down and hitched it to the snowmobile.

"Now, Marya, here are Howie's pills," Mr. Savela said, taking two medicine bottles out of his pocket. "Don't forget to give them to him. He has to take them every day or he gets terribly crippled up with his gout — can't walk at all. I wish he'd move into town for the winter, but he won't leave his cabin."

"I won't forget about the pills," promised Marya. "I'll keep them in this pack with my survival kit." She tucked the medicine bottles into a special pocket in one of the smaller packsacks. "Now, where's *Eric*! We won't be out there before dark if we don't get started!"

"*I'm* here!" Anna wanted to shout. "*I'm* ready to go!" But she kept quiet, because just at that moment Eric appeared on the back porch, with a silly grin on his face.

"Come on, Eric, I'm ready to go!" called Marya. She flung her leg over the seat of the snowmobile, ready to start the engine.

"Coming!" shouted Eric, and half fell down the steps.

Anna watched him flopping across the snow. "Something's wrong," she thought. "What's making him walk like that?"

Eric looked like a clown wearing shoes that were much too big for him.

"That's it! His boots are too big for him," Anna said to herself. "He's wearing Mom's snowmobile boots!"

Eric reached the loaded sled. He called to Marya, "Hey, can I ride back here on the sled? That would be fun!"

"He can't go with those stupid boots on," Anna thought desperately. "Marya will see them and make him stay."

But Marya was in too much of a hurry to notice Eric's feet. "I guess you can ride on the sled," she said impatiently, "but you'll have to hold on when we go over bumps."

"He'll help to steady your load a bit," said Mr. Savela.

12

"That's me, Steady Eddy, at your service," cried Eric, as he climbed on the sled.

"They just *can't* go without me!" Anna thought.

But now the snowmobile started with a tremendous roar. Marya put it in gear, and slowly it pulled away.

"You can't go without me!" Anna cried, but nobody heard her. She stared at the slowly moving snowmobile and at Eric, sitting on the sled. There *was* room for her behind Marya now that Eric was on the sled. But there was no time to tell anyone or to argue.

Anna raced after the snowmobile and flung herself on behind her sister.

Marya turned around in surprise. She stopped the machine, leaving the engine running.

"I'm coming too," said Anna in a loud, determined voice.

Mr. Savela came limping up to them. "Hey," he shouted. "What's going on?"

"I'm going too," said Anna again. She held on tightly to Marya's jacket.

"It's O.K. with me," grinned Marya.

Mr. Savela smiled at his daughters. "Well, all right," he said. "Go along, Anna, and remember, Marya, if it starts to snow, stay at Howie's overnight. *Don't* try to get back. You know all the safety rules about travelling in winter. Don't forget them! Off you go, now — and be careful."

Marya gunned the engine, and the snow-mobile leaped forward.

Anna felt ready to explode with joy. She was going to the Martin Bird. The sparkling winter day seemed to dance with adventure as she and Marya and Eric sped down the snow-covered street towards the bush.

2

Into the Bush

As the snowmobile raced down Second Street, Anna could see the big hill that everyone called Miner's Mountain. It was dead ahead.

"Do we have to climb that?" she called to Marya. The wind seemed to whip the words out of her mouth and blow them away, but Marya heard her and nodded.

"The old bush road to the Martin Bird goes straight up the middle," she yelled. "Hold on. It's going to be exciting!"

Anna turned around to make sure that Eric was all right. He was holding on to both sides of the sled and grinning.

The bush trail was hidden by the week's heavy snowfall. There was a huge bank of snow at the end of Second Street, where the trail began.

Marya had to know the exact place to gun her machine up and over that snowbank. She hit the trail dead on! Then she headed for Miner's Mountain at top speed.

They zoomed up the hill. Eric flipped and flopped on his sled and held on for dear life. Above the engine's roar, Anna could hear him laughing and singing.

"Whoops — hey!" Bursts of laughter. "Oh my DARling, oh my DARling, oh my DARling Clem-EN-tine!"

They hit a tremendous bump that almost sent Eric flying off the sled. The snowmobile shot into the air.

Anna giggled as they landed with a THUMP! She could hear Eric yelling like a bronco rider, "Wheee-Heeee! Ride 'em cowboy!"

The next part of the hill was much steeper, and the snowmobile seemed to be climbing straight up into the sky. Anna felt as if she were clinging to a horse that had reared up on its hind legs. Would the machine tip over backwards and fall right off the mountain? If it didn't, would it ever be able to reach the top? As the engine groaned and snorted, Anna screwed her eyes shut and held on.

At last Anna felt the snowmobile right itself. She didn't have to hang on so tightly. Suddenly the engine stopped, and Anna opened her eyes. They were at the top of Miner's Mountain, on level ground.

"Time to check my load," said Marya, as she hopped off. "How did you like that?"

"It was great!" Eric yelled. "I didn't think we were going to make it!"

Both his sisters laughed when they saw Eric. All the snow flying back from the snowmobile had covered him from eyebrows to boots.

"You look like a snow monster!" laughed Anna.

Marya looked with satisfaction at the neat track behind them. The skis of her machine had carved it on the hill.

"This used to be the road to the Martin Bird mine," she said. "When I was a kid, Howie Stern used to drive his big black car down this hill in the summer. We'd see a huge cloud of dust, and then all the kids would race out to meet him and see the Queen's limousine."

"Did Howie Stern really have a car that belonged to the Queen?" Anna asked.

"He certainly did," Marya answered. "The Queen used it on a Royal visit, and Howie bought it at a sale. But he hasn't driven it for years. Dad says that Howie hit a moose one night as he was driving back from town. He tore the top right off the car and he could have been killed. Nobody's seen the Queen's limousine since! And Howie just keeps to himself out at the old mine."

Anna was quiet for a moment, thinking about the shiny black car purring through the forests.

"What happened to the moose?" she finally asked.

Marya laughed. "You and your animals, Anna. I don't know — the moose hasn't been seen since either!"

Eric was still scraping snow off his face and looking down at the view. The whole little town of Strange Lake was spread out beneath them. They could see the fish shacks, far out on the frozen lake. "Look," said Eric, "you can even see the Strange Lake Mine from here!"

"Do you kids remember when the mine was open?" Marya asked.

"Do I remember, do I *remember*!" said Eric, rolling his eyes. "Everybody walked around with gold nuggets in their pockets. There were hotels on every corner, and . . ."

Anna laughed. "He doesn't remember — he was only three years old when the mine closed. He's just heard what everybody says!"

"But he's right!" Marya said. "Things were a lot different when the mine was open. Everybody had jobs and . . ."

She didn't finish her sentence because Eric had grabbed her arm and was shaking it, hard. "Look down there!" he cried, pointing down the hill. "What's that?"

At the bottom of the hill, where Eric was pointing, Anna and Marya saw a strange snow machine coming along Second Street. Even from the top of the hill they could see that it was large and powerful. There were two men inside.

"That's one of those double-track bushmobiles I've read about!" said Marya. "They can go anywhere."

"Who has a big machine like that in Strange Lake?" asked Eric.

"Nobody," answered Marya. "They must be visitors."

The three young people stared at the yellow machine.

"It looks as if they're headed into the bush!" said Anna, and she was right. She and Marya and

Eric watched from the top of Miner's Mountain
until the big snowmobile had rumbled into the
spruce trees at the bottom of the hill, and
disappeared.

"I think they headed south," said Eric.

"Well, there's no use standing here and
talking about it," said Marya. "C'mon, kids,
we've got a job to do.

"Hop on, Eric. Let's go, Anna — up behind
me. I mustn't let the snowmobile sit with all this
snow in its engine. It might freeze, and then we
wouldn't be able to get it started!"

Marya gave the starter cord a rip. Eric and Anna climbed aboard, and off they went down the trail through the trees.

Riding through the bush was even more beautiful than Anna had imagined it. Every rock and tree wore a thick cap of snow. Ice waterfalls hung from the rock cliffs that they passed. They went round a big bend, and Anna leaned to one side to help the snowmobile make the corner.

It was right then, when she was enjoying herself so much, that the trouble started.

Anna turned around to see if Eric was having fun too — and he wasn't there! There was the sled, bouncing over the bumps behind them, but no Eric.

"Eric!" Anna screamed, but no one could hear over the roar of the snowmobile. Frantically Anna pulled at Marya's sleeve.

Marya turned to see what was wrong. When she saw the empty sled, she cut the engine dead. Suddenly there was silence.

"What happened?" Marya asked.

"I don't know. I just turned around, and Eric wasn't there!" Anna said.

Marya jumped off the snowmobile. "He must have fallen off," she said, sounding worried. "I can't turn the snowmobile around on the trail. We'll have to walk back and find him. I hope he didn't hurt himself!"

They found Eric two minutes later around the corner of a big rock. He was lying just a few metres off the trail, up to his neck in snow. He

was humming the "Crispy Critturs" song from TV.

"I wondered when you'd notice that I'd fallen off," he said, when he saw them coming.

"What happened?" Anna asked.

"You took that corner too fast — and I just flew off," Eric said. "And now I can't get out."

"What do you mean, you can't get out? Are you hurt?" Marya asked.

"Are you kidding? How could I hurt myself landing in all this fluffy white stuff?" Eric waved his arms at the snow. "I'm just stuck, that's all. Plain stuck."

"Can you move your legs?" asked Marya.

"I can wiggle them, but I can't get them out," Eric said. "One of my boots is caught under a branch or something."

"Is he just fooling us?" Anna asked. "Could he really get stuck like that?"

Marya nodded. "I've never seen such deep, powdery snow as this winter," she said. "There's no crust on the snow, especially back in the bush like this. You just sink right down. One step off the trail, and you're up to your neck!"

"Are you two just going to talk, or are you going to get me out of here?" Eric wanted to know.

"We're going to get you out," Marya sighed. "Try falling forward, Eric, and then kick up with your feet."

Eric did a clown fall, face first, without using his hands. When he did stick his hands in front of him, his arms sank to his shoulders. Marya and Anna could see him wiggling and struggling to get his legs free. At last he lifted a snowy face.

"Still stuck," he announced.

"O.K.," said Marya. "We'll have to pull you forward a bit till your feet are free." She broke off a pine-tree branch and held it out to Eric. "Can you reach that? . . . Hold on tight. . . . We'll pull."

Anna and Marya pulled on one end of the branch, and Eric held on and wiggled at the other end.

"Hey, my foot's free!" he shouted suddenly.

"Good," said Marya. "Now, don't try to stand up and walk; just keep crawling forward on your stomach. Pretend you're a snake."

Eric crept and plunged and wiggled through the deep snow until the girls could reach his hands. Then they gave a heave — and Eric was kneeling on the trail, panting.

"I never thought walking through a little snow could be such hard work!" he grunted.

"You can't take a step off the trail without snowshoes, just remember that," said Marya. "Let's get back to the machine."

She strode ahead up the trail, and Anna could tell that she was anxious about getting to Howie's cabin.

"I don't believe you *flew* off, Eric, and I'll bet Marya doesn't either," Anna said in a low voice, as she and Eric hurried to keep up to their sister.

"Well, I sort of fell on purpose," Eric admitted. "I thought it would be fun ... you know...to fall in the snow, and then run after you two and jump on the sled again. I didn't think I'd get stuck!"

Anna shook her head in disgust. People were always saying that she was too serious. For Eric, however, *everything* seemed to be a big joke. She hoped he had learned his lesson.

3

Slush and Snowshoes

The snowmobile bounced over the rough trail. "It's like riding a bucking horse," Anna thought. The wind was blowing in her face, and she was beginning to feel cold. She turned around every few seconds to make sure that Eric was still there. He made terrible faces at her but seemed to be holding on tightly.

"How much farther is it?" Anna had to shout to make Marya hear.

"Another three kilometres, at least," Marya shouted back. "We have to go across the beaver pond here."

The beaver pond looked like any other stretch of snow. In the centre was a big, snow-covered dome that was the beavers' house.

Marya stopped the snowmobile again.

"I just have to check the ice before we cross — Dad says the pond sometimes gets slushy under the snow. You two stay here." Marya walked carefully forward on the trail, looking back at each footstep.

"What's she looking for?" Anna wondered.

"I don't know, but I'm going to find out!" Eric cried.

"Eric! Come back here," shouted Marya, as Eric ran past her, out onto the surface of the pond.

Eric stopped. When he turned around, he had the strangest look on his face.

"Help!" he shouted. "There's water! I'm falling through the ice! I'm drowning!"

"Get back here, you idiot. You're not falling through — that's just slush! But don't fall down in it, whatever you do," cried Marya, sounding really angry.

Eric stumbled towards his sisters. He still had a frightened look on his face. He stopped to look back at his footprints, and almost fell.

"Hurry, Eric! Try to step lightly," Marya urged.

"Step lightly! I can't — my feet feel like lead," Eric shouted.

Anna saw that the slushy ice had frozen on Eric's boots. Now, each one was twice its size.

"Keep trying. Come on. Hurry!" urged Marya. She reached out her hand to her brother.

Every time Eric took a step, his footprint filled up with black, icy water.

"Hurry!" cried Marya again. "You can make it."

Eric's face was red from his frantic efforts. Grimly he plunged through the slush to reach Marya's outstretched hand.

"Oh, boy!" he gasped. "I thought I'd never get out of there. My feet feel as if they're covered in cement."

Anna stared at Eric's feet in amazement. "How did the ice stick like that?" she asked, looking at the huge blobs of ice on each boot.

"It wasn't ice!" said Eric in a strangely quiet voice. "It was water — under the snow."

"It freezes as soon as the air hits it — don't forget that's cold water," said Marya.

26

She straightened up and looked hard at her young brother. "O.K., Eric. You've got to stop charging off on your own when you don't know what you're doing!"

"I'm sorry, Marya," Eric said, sounding as though he really meant it. "I've heard about slush on the ice before — but I didn't know it was like *that*." Eric shivered as he looked back at the dark trail of his footsteps.

"Well, at least you've proved one thing," Marya said. "We can't go across the pond. There's sixty centimetres of good ice underneath the slush, but just imagine what would happen if I drove the snowmobile in there."

"How are we going to get to the Martin Bird mine then?" Anna asked. She was trying hard not to shiver inside her three sweaters and her snowmobile suit. When they were standing around like this, the cold seemed to creep inside her clothes and stay there.

Marya was staring out at the pond. "Well, I can't follow Dad's trail across," she said slowly, "but there's the summer road."

"The summer road! Of course!" shouted Eric.

"Be quiet, Eric, and let me think," said Marya. "I'll have to make a new trail if I take the summer road. That's going to be awfully hard in this deep snow."

She took a map out of her pocket and spread it on the snowmobile seat. "Here we are," she said, pointing to a place on the map where a thick dotted line crossed a marsh. "The summer road follows the edge of the pond and then crosses Beaver Creek on that bridge below the beaver dam."

"But that's a long way!" Eric said.

"It wouldn't be so bad if we didn't have the sled," Marya said.

She thought for a minute.

"I know," she said. "You two kids can take the shortcut across the pond on snowshoes. It will be easier to break trail without passengers, and I'll leave the sled here."

Quickly Marya unbuckled the snowshoes from the back of the snowmobile. "We should have brought an extra pair for you, Anna," she said, "but it doesn't matter. I won't need them. Here — you can wear Eric's, and he can wear mine."

"Are you kidding? Me walk out on that beaver pond again in that STUFF! No way, nothing doing, count me out, unh-uh!" Eric shook his head so hard the tassel almost flew off his hat.

"Don't worry. With the snowshoes you should stay on top of the snow," said Marya.

"Come on, Eric," Anna said, squatting down to do up her snowshoes. "You know Marya wouldn't let us do it if it were dangerous."

"Are you calling me chicken or something?" Eric yelled. "You don't know what it's like out there in that gushy, slushy stuff!"

Anna finished doing up her straps and took a few steps out onto the pond.

"That's far enough!" Marya cried. "Look back. Are your tracks filling up with water?"

Anna turned around and looked down. She could see the big print of the snowshoe clearly. It was nice and dry. "No," she said, "I'm not sinking in very far."

"O.K., Eric, you try. You're heavier," said Marya, handing Eric her snowshoes.

"Is that an order, m'am?" asked Eric sadly.

"Yes, Steady Eddy, that's an order!" replied Marya seriously. It was hard to stay mad at Eric.

Eric did up his straps with a sigh.

"O.K., here I go," he said. "This is a suicide mission if ever there was one. If I never come back, you can have my pet rock to remember me by."

He stepped onto the ice, swinging his legs out wide, the way you have to do to walk in snowshoes.

"Hey, these are magic! I don't sink! Even in my big boots!" yelled Eric. "I can walk on water."

"Good," said Marya. "Now, come back." She was undoing the load on the sled. She put tea, sugar, a can of milk, and some cookies into a small pack.

"Here, Anna," she said. "These are emergency rations in case you get to Howie's cabin first."

Then Marya fished in the packsack in which she'd put the two bottles of medicine. "Stuff this bottle into your pocket, Eric," she said. "That's the medicine the doctor sent out for Howie Stern. I'll keep the second bottle in this packsack with my survival kit. I'll take it and the rest of the supplies behind me on the snowmobile.''

Anna felt her teeth starting to chatter and wished they could get going. The sun had gone behind a lot of clouds.

Marya saw Anna glance up at the gray sky and looked up too. ''I think the snow will hold off until tonight,'' she said.

''You can't get lost,'' Marya continued. She pointed to the opposite shore of the beaver pond. ''See that big jack pine? That's where the trail cuts through the trees. The old Martin Bird mine is just over that hill.''

''When will you be there?'' Anna asked. She knew she'd be a little bit afraid to go into Howie Stern's cabin without Marya, even with Eric for company.

''We should all arrive about the same time,'' said Marya. ''It's a lot farther going *around* the beaver pond than across it, and I'll have to break trail. But I'll still be driving faster than you can walk.

''Just keep to the trail and you'll be fine. Remember, Eric, no more nonsense,'' said Marya, looking sternly at her brother. ''Get started now; I want to make sure your snowshoes are all right.''

Marya watched as Eric and Anna started out across the beaver pond. The slush ended two metres from shore, and, from there on, the ice was dry and hard.

Marya hopped on the big orange snowmobile

and started the motor. She stood up and leaned forward to make the turn onto the summer road.

The machine plowed into the deep snow at top speed. It groaned and moaned, but kept on going.

"This is going to be interesting," thought Marya. "I hope I don't get stuck!"

Howie's Cabin

Eric and Anna looked down at the old Martin Bird mine.

"Wow!" said Eric. "Isn't that something?" His sister nodded her head.

Anna was tired after their long walk across the beaver pond and up the hill — walking on snowshoes was hard work. But at least she was warm, right to her fingers and toes.

"I'd rather walk on snowshoes than sit on a snowmobile and freeze," she thought.

Anna looked at the wood buildings and tumbled-down shacks below them. "Do you think Howie Stern will be glad to see us?" she asked Eric.

"Of course he will. Anyway, I'll sure be glad to see *him*, and get warmed up in his famous log cabin," Eric said.

"How will we know which place is his?" Anna asked. She was still feeling shy and fearful about meeting the old man. "It looks as if there are a lot of cabins," she added, as they started down the trail towards the Martin Bird.

"That's simple," Eric replied. "It'll be the only cabin with smoke coming out of the chimney. Nobody else lives here, you know."

Anna stopped dead in her tracks. She looked down again at the old gray buildings. "But Eric," she said, "there's no smoke coming out of *any* of the chimneys!"

"What?" Eric stopped too, and stared. He looked carefully across the valley below for thin, wispy smoke that Anna might have missed. Everything was perfectly still. Nothing moved or made a sound. Eric and Anna could hear their own hearts beating. They seemed to be the only living things in the whole, great, silent wilderness.

"You're right!" Eric finally admitted. "There's no smoke."

Eric and Anna took off down the hill as fast as they could move on their snowshoes. They had lived all their lives in this north country. They knew, without having to say it, that no fire meant no life. A chimney without smoke meant that the wood fire was out, and nobody could live for long in the winter in a cabin without heat.

The old mine was a strange place. Anna had imagined Howie Stern's cabin standing all alone in a clearing, with trees around the clearing. Now she realized that there had been a little town here.

Over the door of a tall, narrow building, with its windows boarded up, Anna saw a sign that said:
MARTIN BIRD CHURCH
"Look, Eric, they even had a church here." Her voice sounded loud and funny in the silence.

There were lots of other, smaller buildings beyond the church. All of them were leaning crazily into snowbanks, with deep drifts covering half their windows and doors.

Eric and Anna walked down the street of the little town. Tall evergreen trees stood like silent soldiers behind the old gray buildings.

"How will we find Howie Stern's house?" Anna asked again.

"It's a log cabin," Eric replied, almost whispering. "Look, Anna. There it is!"

Sure enough, there was a neat log cabin. It wasn't all alone in a clearing, as Anna had pictured it, but it *was* set a little back from the other houses, and it had trees on three sides. The front porch was shovelled clean, and a prospector's packsack hung on a hook just outside the door. But there was not a sliver of smoke coming out of the big chimney.

"Maybe we shouldn't go in," Anna said slowly. "Maybe we should wait for Marya." She knew as she said it that she didn't sound very brave.

"No. Come on, Anna, don't be scared. We have to go in." Eric grasped her hand in its thick snowmobile mitt and pulled her after him. "We came to help Howie Stern, remember?"

"But what if he's . . . if he's, . . . " Anna couldn't finish her sentence.

"Whatever's wrong, we have to find out," Eric said. His voice seemed terribly loud, now that he'd stopped whispering. He hoped that he

34

sounded braver than he felt. He stomped up to the porch in his snowshoes and pounded on the door.

Anna and Eric waited, holding their breath, listening to their pounding hearts. No one shouted, "Come in." Nothing moved inside.

Eric pounded again. He called, "Mr. Stern, Mr. Stern, are you home?" There was no answer.

"Maybe he's not home," said Eric.

Anna pointed to a pair of snowshoes leaning against the wall.

"Well," said Eric, "maybe those are his best snowshoes. Maybe he went somewhere on his second-best snowshoes. I'm going to look in the window."

Eric brushed the snow from the cabin window. A black face with two bright yellow eyes looked out through the clear spot he had made.

Eric almost fell over his snowshoes in surprise and fright.

"That's Toby, the cat!" Anna cried.

"Boy, did he give me a shock!" said Eric.

Anna came up on the porch and peered in the window too. She could hear Toby meowing behind the glass.

Eric was unstrapping his snowshoes. He stamped the snow off his boots. "Are you coming, Anna?" he asked.

"I guess so," she said, "but I sure wish Marya was here."

Eric pushed gently on the cabin's heavy plank door. It swung open silently. Together, Eric and Anna stepped into the dark room.

The only light came from two small windows on either side of the door.

Anna and Eric stood inside the door, trying to get used to the dim light. They could just make out the gleaming front of the stove, a neat table with plates and cups stacked on it, and a rocking chair covered in an old quilt.

Anna began to shiver. She clamped her teeth together to keep them from chattering.

Toby, the big black cat, hopped down from the window sill and came over to rub against their legs.

As their eyes became used to the shadows, Anna and Eric could see the shape of a huge bed against the back wall. Suddenly they heard a voice coming from the bed.

"Is somebody there? Who opened that door? You let in an icy blast!"

The sound of the voice was so sudden in the silent room that Anna almost jumped out of her skin. She grabbed Eric, then realized that he was holding onto her just as hard. They couldn't see anyone in the bed! Both of them were too frightened to move or speak.

"Who's there?" came the voice again. "What's the matter with you?" The voice sounded old and cross — thin, Anna thought, like watery tea. It didn't sound like the voice of a real person.

"Come over here where I can see you," said the voice impatiently.

Eric and Anna edged towards the bed.

"Well, do you see, Toby, what the Lord sends me in my time of trouble? . . . a pair of crazy little kids."

Toby the cat flashed past them like a black streak and leaped up on the end of the bed.

"Ow! Watch my toe, you fool cat!" howled the voice.

Anna and Eric saw a thin, bony arm shoot out and grab Toby by the scruff of the neck. The arm lowered the cat to the floor.

The children glanced at each other. There *was* a person in the bed!

As they came nearer, Eric and Anna could see a pair of sharp old eyes peering at them from under the covers. That was all there *was* to see of the old man. On his head he wore a thick, black tuque pulled right down to his eyes. The blankets came up to his nose.

"Excuse me, sir. Are you Mr. Stern?" asked Eric in a shaky kind of voice.

"Who do you think I am — Santa Claus?" said the old man crossly.

Anna thought he looked more like the big, bad wolf than Santa Claus, hiding under the covers like that. She was beginning to feel less frightened, though. Howie Stern might be a grouch, but he needed help!

"We brought your medicine and some supplies, Mr. Stern," Anna said. "I'm Anna Savela, and this is my brother Eric. Our sister Marya is coming with the rest of your pills and supplies. She should be here soon."

Eric handed the bottle of pills to the old man. Howie peered at them anxiously and then stared back at Anna and Eric.

"Where's Ray Savela?" he asked. "This is Friday, isn't it? He always comes on Friday."

"Dad hurt his leg," explained Eric. "He couldn't come."

"Well, skin it and fry it!" Howie Stern cried, "so he sent you instead! And me with my stove stone cold since dawn, and my gout so bad I can't set foot out of bed!" He pounded his blankets with a clenched fist. "I sure hope you kids can make a fire in a wood stove, 'cause if you can't, we're all going to freeze as hard as cinders!"

"Sure we can — we've done it hundreds of times," said Eric quickly. "Just tell us where you keep your wood, Mr. Stern."

"Outside on the woodpile, if there's any left," Howie Stern said. "Before you go, get me something to take with these fool pills. Might be some water in that glass on the table."

Anna hurried over to see. There was water in a glass all right, but its surface was covered with a thin layer of ice! Anna gasped. It was really and truly freezing in the cabin!

Howie Stern saw the startled look on her face. "Just break the ice with a knife, and stir it around," he grunted impatiently. "Ice-water will wash down these pills as well as any."

Anna broke the ice and took the glass to Mr. Stern. She shivered as she watched him gulp down his medicine.

"Will you be all right now, sir?" Eric asked, anxiously.

"Right as rabbits — in a few hours," was the reply. "When I'm not having an attack, why, my foot's as good as anybody's. Better than lots."

"Does it hurt now?" Eric wanted to know.

"Hurt! Take a look at this toe!" answered the old man, pulling the blankets away from his feet. "But don't breathe too hard on her. Even the draft from the door feels like flames lickin' at my foot!"

Eric and Anna sucked in their breath and bent closer. Over one of Howie Stern's feet was a thing like a wire cage.

"What's that?" breathed Eric in amazement, staring at the cage.

"Can't stand the touch of the sheets," explained the prospector, "so I cut the top off my old bird cage. Use to belong to a budgie named Petey — a good friend of Toby's and mine, until he died."

Anna and Eric could see Howie Stern's bare foot inside the cage. The big toe was all swollen and red.

"I can't stand up, and I couldn't get my boot on that crazy-looking foot even if I could get out of bed," the old man complained. "You'll have to get the wood, and split it, and get the stove fired up yourselves, you young'uns. I sure am glad you've had lots of experience."

"Yes, sir! Don't you worry; we'll have this cabin warm as toast in a minute," said Eric, moving toward the door.

Anna followed him. "Eric!" she whispered fiercely, "why do you keep on saying we know all about wood stoves! We've never made a fire in a wood stove in our lives!"

5

Dampers and Drafts

"Stop being such a worry-worm!" said Eric. "We'll get a fire going." He had found the axe and was splitting birch logs on Howie Stern's front porch.

"I hope so," Anna answered. At least they knew how to split the wood. They had learned that from their parents on their camping trips.

Anna began to shiver from head to foot. She had to keep moving to keep warm. Now, her clothes seemed to be freezing against her skin.

"You look a little cold," Eric said, noticing Anna's blue lips. "Here, do some work for a change. That will warm you up!" He handed Anna the axe.

Anna swung at the log but missed. Her arms were so stiff with cold that she couldn't aim the axe properly.

"Not like that!" shouted Eric. "You know better than that. You'll cut off your leg if you aren't careful."

"I'll go and get some more logs," Anna said. She handed the axe back to Eric and went around the side of the cabin. That's where they had found Howie's woodpile, neatly stacked under the slanting eaves.

Anna thought she had never felt so cold. Shuddering, she picked up a load of logs and plunged through the snow back to the porch. That warmed her up a little bit.

"Let me try again," she said to Eric. "It's either that or turn into an icicle!" She swung the axe high and whipped it down with a quick motion of her wrists. This time the log split neatly in two.

Anna split a few more logs and began to feel less shivery. Then she split some of the half logs into thinner pieces for kindling.

"That's enough," sang out Eric. "We're not splitting wood for the whole town."

Anna put down the axe reluctantly. She was feeling so much better that she hated to stop. "All right," she said, "but I hope we can make that stove work." She picked up an armful of wood and followed Eric inside.

As they dropped the wood into the wood box, Howie appeared from under his mound of blankets. His tuque was over one eye.

"I see you found my woodpile," he grunted. "Now don't forget to open the damper and close the draft before you start her up!"

"We won't," called Eric cheerfully.

"What's he talking about?" whispered Anna, staring at the stove.

"All these knobs and levers here," Eric answered, pushing and pulling everything that moved.

"Matches are in the warming oven, in a jar," went on the old man, calling instructions from his bed.

"Warming oven?" puzzled Eric. He opened the oven door.

"No, not that! . . . the *warming* oven," sputtered Howie Stern. "Up above; look up!"

Eric had started to wave his arms and jump around, the way he did when he felt helpless. But Anna reached up on tiptoes and pulled down a flap. Inside was a thing like a cupboard, and there sat the matches, in a glass jar.

"Here," she said. "C'mon, Eric, get a grip on yourself. We've got to get this fire going." She was starting to shiver again.

"We need newspaper," said Eric.

"Don't get a newspaper out here!" snorted Howie Stern. "You'll have to make yourself a starter stick."

"Starter stick?" Eric almost shouted. "What's a *starter stick*?"

"Bring me a skinny piece of wood and a sharp knife and I'll show you," said Howie, sitting up and making his bedsprings squeak.

He showed them how to shave little pieces at the end of a stick so that it stuck out all around like a Halloween cat's tail. "Those little shavings will catch your flame like a piece of paper," he explained.

Eric carried the precious starter stick as if it were the Olympic torch. He stuck his hand right down inside the round hole on top of the stove and carefully laid wood around the stick. He reached for a match without taking his eyes off it.

"Hurry, Eric," urged Anna. "I'm freezing."

"This-has-got-to-be-done-right," said Eric slowly. He struck the match on the top of the stove and poked it down the hole.

"It's going; it's going!" he shouted, leaping into the air.

"Don't you think you should put the lid back on?" asked Anna nervously, as flames danced out of the top of the stove.

"No, I want to watch my beautiful fire," said Eric. "It's going . . . it's going . . . it's going . . . *out*!" he howled. "What's the matter with this dumb stove? My fire's going out!" The flames had disappeared.

Howie Stern bounced impatiently on his bedsprings. "Skin and fry this fool toe!" he cried, "I can't see what you're doing from here. Did you open the draft down near the bottom on the other side, son?"

"Draft! What draft? Where?" moaned Eric, as his fire died lower and lower.

Anna quickly squatted down beside the stove, poking at a knob. "Try this," she suggested, pushing the knob to one side.

"Yippee! It's going again!" Eric cried gleefully, pointing to a cheerful blaze down in the stove. He banged the stove lid on and grinned at

Anna. "I think we licked her!" he crowed. There was a big streak of soot down his nose.

"What about the smoke, Eric?" Anna asked. Smoke was pouring from every crack in the stove.

Eric stared at it. He lifted the lid again, and a

huge cloud of smoke billowed into his face. Choking and sputtering, he managed to slide the lid back in place. He fanned at the smoke with his hands and blew at it. But the smoke didn't stop.

"Are you trying to burn my place down?" roared Howie from the bed. "Open the chimney damper!"

By now Eric was almost in tears. "I don't know what a chimney damper is!" he wailed. "This dumb stove has more parts than a Chinese puzzle!"

They heard a chuckle and a cough from the bed. "Just give that little spring thing on the stove pipe half a twist before we're smoked out of here," Howie said. "That way the smoke can get up the chimney."

Eric reached for the spring and twisted it. He felt something move inside the pipe. Almost like magic the stove stopped smoking. Eric waited a moment, expecting that something else would go wrong. "If I turn my back on that stove, it'll probably *explode* or something," he moaned.

Howie Stern was still laughing. "No, it'll work like a wonder now," he chuckled. "But next time you fire up a wood stove, try to get your dampers and your drafts straight, son."

In less than an hour, the fire was burning merrily, and smoke rose in a steady column from Howie's chimney. Inside the cabin, it was beginning to warm up.

"It takes a long time to heat up a log house," Howie Stern explained. "The logs soak

46

up the heat — but then it stays warm a lot longer too.''

Eric went out into the cold again to get snow to melt for tea. When it was ready, he and Anna unpacked their sugar and canned milk and pulled two stools over by Howie's bed.

Anna put the cookies on a plate, and Eric poured steaming hot tea from the old metal teapot. Howie Stern smiled a real smile as he took his first sip of tea.

"It must have been hours since he's had anything warm to drink," thought Anna.

Toby the cat had *his* saucer of hot tea — with no milk — on the floor beside the bed. He was purring happily as he lapped it away.

"Yes, sir," said Howie. "Your dad couldn't do better himself. You're a mighty fine pair of kids!" His old eyes shone at them. "Now, what did you say about the rest of my supplies . . . did you say they were coming out with someone else?"

Anna and Eric looked at each other in horror. They had been so busy with the wood and the fire and making the tea that they had forgotten all about Marya! Where was she?

"What's the matter?" asked the old man, seeing the frightened looks on their faces.

"Our sister Marya . . . ," said Eric. "She came around by the summer road — on the snow-mobile. She should be here by now!"

Howie's face grew very serious. "Now that's a mistake," he said, "trying to bring a snowmobile around the pond. Didn't she know there's no trail broken there?''

"She knew," said Eric, growing more worried by the second, "but she couldn't get across the pond because of the slush."

The old man shook his head. "Mighty tough job, breaking trail with a snowmobile this time of year, with this much snow," he said.

"Oh, Marya's very experienced in the bush," Anna said.

"It's still a mighty tough job!" said Howie. "I suppose, though, if she got herself stuck with the machine, she'd come on with her snowshoes. Maybe that's what's taking her a little extra time. You two young ones haven't been here that long, you know — just about an hour. Seems like a long time, when you're fighting the cold and trying to get a fire going, but it hasn't been that long."

Eric and Anna weren't listening. They were staring at each other with a great fear on their faces.

"Eric," said Anna in a frightened whisper, "you've got Marya's snowshoes . . . and I've got yours!"

They both turned to look at Howie Stern. "Marya hasn't got any snowshoes, sir, " Eric said slowly. "We brought Anna at the last minute and we only packed two pairs . . . "

Anna felt numb with fear. She wanted to cry, but her tears were frozen behind her eyelids. If she hadn't come, Marya wouldn't be out there in the deep snow with no snowshoes!

"Listen, Anna," Eric said, "we don't even know that the snowmobile broke down. Maybe Marya's just going slowly....Like Mr. Stern said, we haven't been here as long as it feels."

He tried to sound cheerful, but he was remembering how awful and helpless he had felt when he couldn't move in the deep snow after he fell off the sled.

The old man in the bed shook his head. "Doesn't sound to me like you had this trip very well planned. I hope you're right, son, and that your sister's just taking it slow. There's no trail out there, and it's getting almighty cold. You make one mistake in this country and you don't get a chance to make another one."

Anna squeezed her eyes tight together. She was trying to block out a terrible picture. In her mind she could see Marya struggling through the snow, with night coming and the temperature falling.

"I sure was anxious to get those supplies," Howie Stern sighed. "There's something your dad was bringing that was mighty important. I was going to get your dad to ... " The old man sank back on his pillow. "Well, I guess it's probably too late now, anyway."

Eric stood up. "I'm going to find her!" he said. "I've still got all afternoon and at least two or three hours of daylight. It isn't more than a few kilometres down to the bridge over Beaver Creek." Eric's mind went racing ahead, planning the rescue.

"I'll need to take an extra pair of snowshoes for Marya," he said. "Can I borrow a pair of yours, Mr. Stern?"

"Lots of extras in that cupboard beside the door. Take a small pair," said the prospector. "Hate to see you go, son,...and all by yourself.... Sure wish I was on my pins and could go with you. It's a bad business going out there alone. But if your sister's out there somewhere ... and without snowshoes ... "

"I'm going too," said Anna suddenly, in a determined voice.

Eric stopped on his way to the door and looked at his little sister. Anna had a very firm lift to her chin as she stared back at him.

"You should stay here where it's warm," Eric said.

"I'm going," repeated Anna, and tried not to shudder inside. She knew it would be very, very cold out there. They might not come back for a long time. She pressed her lips tight together so that Eric wouldn't see how scared she was of freezing.

Eric knew from experience how stubborn Anna could be. "All right," he said. "Come on, then; get ready."

"You'll find the road easily enough," said Howie Stern from his pillows. "Used to be a good road, once upon a time. Just turn at the church and go south between the two big pines. But don't go wandering off the road, and get back here before dark. I don't want you lost too."

6

Find Marya!

Out in the cold, Anna and Eric plodded through the snow. Anna was leading. Eric was still having trouble with those enormous boots of his.

Anna lifted her snowshoes forward in a steady stride. Two words pounded in her head and kept her feet going: Find Marya! Find Marya! Find Marya! . . .

"Anna, will you slow down a little!" shouted Eric.

Anna looked over her shoulder and saw Eric away down the trail, fumbling with his straps again. "Come on, Eric, you're slower than a turtle," she called back.

Anna kept on walking. If Marya had had an accident, she wanted to get to her fast.

"Well, it isn't going to help if you get lost too!" shouted Eric. "Wait for me!" If only he could walk faster on these stupid snowshoes! In his mother's boots, Marya's snowshoes, and with the extra pair strapped on his back, it wasn't easy!

The snow began. It fell softly, in big flakes, making no sound in the silent forest.

Anna licked the first flakes off her top lip as the snow hit her face.

"Anna!" Eric panted up behind her. "You're a speed demon. Slow down!"

"Look at the snow, Eric," Anna said. The flakes were now coming down thick and fast. "How are we going to find Marya if it keeps on snowing like this?"

"If she's on this trail, and we're on this trail, we'll bump into each other some time," Eric said, "even if we can't see our noses in front of our faces."

"But what if Marya's not on the trail?" Anna said anxiously.

"That's what worries me, too," her brother agreed.

"I'm not going back until we find her," Anna said, marching through the snow.

Eric shook his head and followed. He wished his sister wouldn't say things like that. He knew she meant it, even if they had to walk all night.

"After we find Marya," Eric thought, "we have to find our way back. How will we do that if the snow keeps falling?" Eric turned around to look at the tracks he was making with his snowshoes. Already they were filling in. In just a few more minutes they would disappear completely.

Eric began to break branches off the low spruce trees beside the old road. He stuck them into the snow as he walked. "Just in case," he thought, "it gets dark, or the snowstorm turns into a *real* blizzard." Every few metres Eric stuck another branch into the snow.

Marking the trail slowed Eric down even more. Soon Anna was far ahead of him again. She could hear nothing in the great forest, and the world she could see was getting smaller and smaller. She felt as if she was wrapped in a thick blanket of snow.

All of a sudden, through the thick, white snow before her, she saw a ghostly shape.

"Eric," she whispered, turning her head slightly and reaching back — but Eric wasn't there.

The shape in front of her didn't move. It was gray and white, like the snow, and Anna wasn't even sure that she was really seeing anything.

She took another step forward. The shape moved and lifted its head. Anna gasped. She saw two glowing, yellow eyes looking at her, and two sharp, pointed ears with long, black ear tufts. A large animal was crouching in the snow, right in front of her!

It seemed to Anna that she and the animal stared at each other forever. The animal's thick, soft fur was almost covered in snow. Its huge furry paw was outstretched. Anna saw that underneath the paw was another white shape, almost buried in the snow.

It was the body of a snowshoe rabbit.

Anna was too scared to breathe. She knew what the animal was now.

It was a lynx! Her dad had told her that the lynx was one of the fiercest animals in the bush. It could even kill a deer, he had said. And here she was, only a few steps away from one! She had surprised it by coming so quietly through the snow. The lynx must have just killed that rabbit for its dinner, and she had interrupted it.

"Maybe if I don't move," Anna thought, "maybe if I just act like I'm part of the forest, it will go back to eating its dinner and leave me alone." She couldn't think of anything else to do!

"Crack!" Far behind her Eric broke off the dead branch of a spruce tree. The lynx leaped to its feet. Anna could see its long legs and huge paws.

"Go away. Shoo! Go away, lynx!" Anna shouted, waving her arms. The lynx crouched back, as if it were going to spring. Then, it seemed to change its mind about jumping at this waving, yelling thing. Instead, it turned and ran. Almost at once it faded out of sight — as if it had melted into the snow.

Anna's heart was pounding, and her breath was coming in great pants, the way it did when she'd been running hard for a long time.

Eric came plodding up, tripping over his snowshoes as usual. "What's the matter?" he asked. "What was all that yelling about?" Then he saw his sister's frightened face. "Hey," he asked, "what scared you?"

Anna pointed to the rabbit.

"A little rabbit?" laughed Eric. "Were you afraid of a little, dead rabbit?"

Anna was still breathless. She shook her head and pointed to the big tracks the lynx had made running away.

Eric whistled in surprise as he bent over to look carefully at the tracks. "I was wrong," he said. "You were afraid of a big, live LYNX!" He started shouting and jumping around. "You could have been attacked!" he screamed. "You were standing *this* close. It could have jumped right at you. Wow ... a lynx!" Eric tripped over his snowshoe and sat down, almost on top of the rabbit.

Anna helped him up. "It got scared when I yelled," she said, finding her breath. "But it might come back to get its dinner. We'd better get going."

"You mean you just yelled at it, and it ran away?" Eric said, amazed. "You're the bravest sister I ever had. I can't believe you did that! Hey, if that wasn't brave!"

"I don't feel very brave now," Anna said, and it was true. She had started to tremble all over.

"Well, come on; you'll soon feel better. Let's stay together this time," Eric said. "But we can't look very much longer, Anna." He looked up at the falling flakes, then down at the trail. "I can't tell where the sun is in the sky, it's snowing so hard."

After what had happened, Anna knew Eric was right. They couldn't stay out in the bush after dark, no matter how much she wanted to find Marya. "Just let her be right over the next hill," Anna prayed. "Just let us find her soon, and let her be all right."

Anna could hardly believe that it was still the same day on which she and Eric and Marya had set out from Strange Lake together. The sun had been shining, and she had been so excited. Now it was getting darker and colder, the snow was falling thicker and faster than ever — and Marya was lost.

7

The Signal from the Cave

"We've got to go back, Anna," Eric said, brushing the snow out of his eyes. "I can hardly see!"

Anna was shivering. "What if Marya needs help, Eric?" she asked. "Can't we go just a little bit farther?"

"No," said Eric. "Not one step. Listen, Anna, Marya will be all right. She knows what she's doing out here in the woods. We don't. We're just kids, and in a minute we're going to be lost, and someone will have to come and save us. Only there isn't anyone *to* come, so we're going back . . . now!"

Anna knew Eric was right. This adventure was getting too big for them. But she had a *feeling,* a deep-down *feeling,* that Marya was somewhere near. She wanted to go on looking just a little bit longer.

"Eric, couldn't we climb a high tree or something . . . and look around?" Anna begged.

"Are you kidding? What am I going to see from a tree that I can't see right here on the ground? Millions of snowflakes, that's all."

The snow stuck to their hoods and their eyebrows; it melted on the ends of their noses. The light was getting dim and gray.

Eric was glad that he had marked their trail with spruce branches. "Come on, Anna," he urged. "For the hundredth time ... let's go back!"

Anna's feeling was stronger than ever. "Eric!" she called.

"What now?"

"See that hill up there? Let's just climb it and look around." Anna pointed to a high ridge of rock above the road. "We could see right around the corner from up there."

Eric stopped and sighed. "O.K.," he said. "We'll climb the hill, and look around, and then we're going back. Promise?"

" I promise," said Anna.

They set off up the hill, climbing over fallen trees and around rocks that stuck up through the snow. It was a steep climb, and Eric was ahead of Anna. He reached for the low bough of a tree and pulled himself up to the top of the ridge.

"Like I said — all I can see is billions of snowflakes!" said Eric, letting go of the branch to wave his arms at the snow. "Snowflakes and ... aggggh!"

Anna never heard the end of the sentence, because Eric disappeared. He let go of the branch that he was holding and shot straight down into the snow.

Anna blinked and rubbed her eyes. It was

impossible. Eric *couldn't* disappear. Puffing and panting, she pulled herself up the last bit of rock to the top.

"Stop!" A voice that Anna didn't recognize came from nowhere. "Don't take another step!" The voice was low and hollow.

"Anna," said the spooky voice, "I . . . I'm down here . . . "

"Eric!" Anna cried. "Is that *you?* Where on earth are you?"

"I'm not *on* earth," came the strange-sounding voice. "I'm under it!"

"It *has* to be Eric," Anna thought. "Nobody else would be making dumb jokes when he's just disappeared.

"What happened, Eric?" she yelled again. "Where are you?"

"Hold onto the tree, tight, and look down here," the voice floated up to her.

Anna wiggled her way carefully up to the tree branch that Eric had been holding. She edged her way forward. Then she gasped. "Oh, Eric, are you down *there?*"

It looked as if the snow had opened up and swallowed him. Far below, in a big, dark hole, Anna could see the top of Eric's hood. He lifted his face, and she could see his blue eyes. The snow was falling on his face, and he looked scared.

"It's an old mine shaft, I think," Eric said. "Lucky for me there's lots of snow in it up this far. I'm standing on snow holding onto an old

ladder or something — I grabbed it on the way
down. But it doesn't look strong enough to hold
my full weight. So how do I get out?''

"I can get you out," Anna said. "Can you
hang on to the ladder while you take off your
snowshoes? Hand the first one up to me. Then I'll
pull you out with the other one.''

Quickly Anna tore off her mitt and undid her own snowshoe straps with shaking hands. She slipped out of her snowshoes, then lay down flat on her stomach at the edge of the hole. As Eric's first snowshoe appeared, she grabbed it and laid it beside her own. When the end of the second snowshoe appeared, Anna gripped it and held on with all her might while Eric used it to climb out of the hole.

"Eric Savela, the things you get into!" Anna cried when he was lying, panting, beside her on the snow. "How do you manage to get into so much trouble?"

"Listen!" Eric panted, ignoring Anna's question. He was still trying to get his breath. "I saw something . . . just before I fell down the hole . . . a light or something . . . look over there!" He pointed through the thick, falling snow.

Anna looked hard, and, at first, she didn't see anything. Then she saw a flicker, an orange spark through the gray. A signal fire!

Eric and Anna went down the hill and along the darkening trail as fast as their snowshoes could carry them. They were sure that the orange glow they had seen through the snow was a signal fire — Marya's signal fire! Now it didn't matter if there were ten blizzards — Marya was close by, and they were going to find her.

Around the next corner, Anna stopped. "Look down there, Eric!" she cried. She pointed to a patch of bright orange against a tree. "There's Dad's snowmobile!"

"Jumping catfish . . . so that's what happened," Eric gasped. "Marya shot off the trail and cracked up against that tree!"

"But where's Marya?" said Anna. "She can't be down there. We saw a fire!"

"Marya!" Eric hollered into the falling snow. "We've come to save you. Where are you, Marya?" Silence.

"Mar-y-a! Mar-y-a! Can you hear us, Marya?" Anna shouted.

Still there was only silence.

"Mar-y-a! MAR-Y-A!" Anna and Eric hollered together.

Suddenly there was another voice.

"I'm up here!" came a glad shout from over their heads.

Eric and Anna looked up , and there was the orange glow again.

They started up the hill, the extra pair of snowshoes flapping on Eric's back. Closer and closer they came to the flickering light. At last, through the trees, they saw the black mouth of a cave, flames leaping from a fire — and Marya!

In no time at all, they were all three stuffed into the cave, hugging each other and warming themselves in front of Marya's fire.

Marya gave Eric a special hug for bringing the snowshoes for her. "Thank you, Steady Eddy," she said. "You'll be glad to get those off your back."

"Sure will," grinned Eric. "I have enough trouble with the ones on my feet."

"Whew! Doesn't it smell awful in here!" said Anna, when she had recovered from her joy at seeing Marya safe and well.

"Isn't that a terrible stink?" laughed Marya. "I think the last person who lived in this cave was an untidy animal."

"What animal?" asked Eric. "A bear?"

"I think it was a lynx," said Marya. "I saw a big gray animal leave when I came close."

"A lynx!" exclaimed Anna. Then she and Eric told Marya about Anna's meeting the lynx on the trail.

"You were lucky to see a lynx that close," said Marya, putting her arm around her young sister and giving her a hug. "They're really shy animals."

"I didn't feel lucky at the time," Anna said, shivering at the memory.

"And then I fell down a mine shaft!" Eric said. "But we'll tell you about that later. Now we want to hear what happened to *you*."

"It's a long story," said Marya. "I'll try to tell you quickly. We should start back before it gets really dark." As she talked, Marya was stuffing her gear back into the packsack. "Wow, am I glad to see you two — even if you shouldn't have come! Now for my story."

8

Marya's Mysteries

"It was hard work, making a new trail," Marya began'— "a lot harder than I expected. The snowmobile kept plunging deep down into the snow, and I had to really blast it through the drifts. My arms ached just from trying to keep it from turning over.

"Then, all of a sudden, it shot ahead so fast that I nearly fell off. It was running on a hard-packed trail!"

"A trail!" said Eric. "A snowmobile trail?"

"A big, wide-track snowmobile trail!" said Marya. "I hopped off to check, and I could feel the ridges of the trail through the snow."

"How did the trail get there?" asked Anna.

"I don't know," Marya replied, "but I kept thinking about that big, yellow snow machine we saw from the top of Miner's Mountain. I hoped the trail would go all the way to Howie's cabin, but it didn't. It stopped at the hill on the other side of the bridge."

"What a weird place for it to end," said Eric.

"It didn't really end there," Marya explained. "It swung off to the south, around the shore of Beaver Creek."

"I wonder where it went," said Anna.

"I wondered that too," said Marya. "I got off the snowmobile and followed the trail a little way, but it disappeared into thick bush. But do you know what? When I looked around, I saw *smoke* rising above the trees in the same direction that the trail led. And there isn't *anything* marked on the map there."

"Where was the smoke coming from?" asked Eric, eagerly.

"I was dying to find out," replied Marya, "but I couldn't take time to explore."

"What a mystery," said Anna, "smoke and an unmarked trail! What did you do next, Marya?"

"I got back on the snowmobile to follow the old trail north to Howie's. It goes up another hill — and was I glad when I finally made it to the top. Then the trail goes along the top of the hill where it overlooks the beaver pond. *That's* where the problems started."

"What happened?" asked Eric. "Hurry up!"

"Just relax," laughed Marya. "I'm hurrying. The snowmobile was trying to hurry too — charging as fast as it could through the deep snow. Suddenly, one of the skis caught on a branch under the snow. The machine flipped over and pitched me off. The next thing I remember, I was lying in a snowbank!"

"Thank goodness for the soft snow," said Anna. "You could have been killed."

"But I wasn't," said Marya. "I wasn't even hurt — just a little stunned. The worst part was when I saw Dad's new snowmobile."

"We saw it just after we saw your fire," said Anna.

"Yes, it's nestled against a pine tree a little way down the slope," sighed Marya. "I feel terrible about it."

"Maybe it's not really damaged," said Eric. "Anyway, Dad will be glad you're O.K."

"At that point I was nearly frozen," said Marya. "I wanted a fire and food and shelter. Most of all I wanted to get to Howie's cabin and make sure you two were O.K."

"But you couldn't get there without snowshoes," said Anna. "Oh, Marya, I felt awful when I remembered that you didn't have any snowshoes — because I came along."

"Never mind," said Marya. "It was my own fault, not yours. Anyway, I had to get the pack with the survival kit in it. *That* was the hardest thing I had to do. I had to wriggle down and back through the snow, the way Eric did when he fell off the sled. While I was down there, I put the fresh vegetables into my pack. They'd freeze on the snowmobile overnight. But Howie's heavy supplies are still on it.

"Finally I struggled back up to the trail with the pack. Then I got my knife out of the survival kit to make a pair of snowshoes. I used small poplar branches for the frames, and wove smaller branches in and out to make the shoe. The snowshoes looked great. Then I took two steps — and sank! The beautiful snowshoes had fallen apart!''

"Weren't you scared?" asked Eric. "Alone out there in all that cold and snow?" He was remembering how he felt when he was stuck in the snowdrift before his sisters came to look for him.

"I didn't let myself think about it," said Marya. "Besides, I was too busy. I had to find a place to spend the night, and get a fire going."

"How did you find this cave?" asked Anna.

"I didn't want to leave the trail," said Marya. " I didn't want to get lost, and without snowshoes I could hardly move in the snow. Then I spotted this big crack in the rock above the trail and struggled through the snow to reach it. That's when I saw the lynx leaving — and I just hoped it would be gone for a long time! I was so glad to have its warm, dry house that I didn't even mind the smell!"

"Did the lynx light the fire for you, too?" asked Eric.

"Not quite," laughed Marya, "but it was thoughtful enough to have its floor covered with dried leaves. They were perfect for starting the fire — after I'd cleared some of the deep snow away from the cave entrance. Luckily, there were dried pine and poplar branches close to the cave, so I didn't have to struggle very far for firewood. At last I had a good fire going and a pile of wood for the night. By the time I'd finished, I was exhausted!"

"Had you been in the cave very long when we arrived?" asked Anna.

"Long enough to think about another mystery," said Marya. "When I'd reached into the pack for my survival kit, I'd heard something jingle in the bottom of the pack. Sitting beside the fire, I decided to find out what had made the noise."

"What was it?" asked Anna.

"It was a wire ring, with flat metal rectangles strung on it," said Marya. "Prospectors' tags!"

"Prospectors' tags!" said Anna. "How did they get in your pack?"

"Dad must have put them there for Howie," said Marya. "But why? That's what I can't understand. Howie has a prospector's licence, of course, and he's always looking for gold . . . "

"Except he can't go looking for it now. The rocks are buried under snow!" said Eric.

"That's exactly what I was thinking when I heard you calling my name," said Marya.

"What a story!" said Anna. "Do you think we'll be able to solve all these mysteries?"

"Maybe Howie will be able to explain them," said Marya, " — at least the one about the prospectors' tags." She stood up and picked up her pack. "Now, if you're rested enough, let's throw some snow on this fire and get going."

Quickly they strapped on their snowshoes, put out the fire, and were ready to go.

"We'll think about the strangers' snowmobile, the mystery trail, and the metal tags on our way to the cabin," said Anna.

"And about that mine shaft I fell down," said Eric.

Marya, Eric, and Anna went down the hill and began the long walk back to the cabin. It was snowing harder than ever. The wind blew snow in their faces and covered up their tracks. They could hardly see or catch their breath. Anna thought how easy it would be to get lost.

Then they came to one of Eric's spruce boughs, stuck in the snow beside the trail, and they knew they were still on the road. Every few metres there was another branch, like a little flag blowing in the wind to show them the way.

"It's a good thing you left those branches to mark the trail!" Marya shouted back to Eric.

"Brilliant, wasn't it?" Eric shouted back.

The three plodded on. Anna was tired again — so tired that she could hardly lift one snowshoe and swing it in front of the other. She felt as if she had been trudging through the snowstorm for most of her life. Up one hill and down another. All the hills and all the corners looked the same through the swift-driving snow.

Anna watched Eric's boots in front of her . . . lift and swing . . . lift and swing. She wondered how poor old Eric could manage in those terrible oversized boots. He must be tired, too, she thought.

He was. All he could think about was the cosy cabin with the fire roaring in the stove and Toby the cat curled up in front of it. "A big mug of tea and about a thousand cookies," Eric thought. "That's all I ask for."

As for Marya, it felt wonderful to have those big, firm snowshoes under her feet. Now she could stride along on top of the snow, instead of wriggling on her stomach, or sinking in up to her thighs with every step. She didn't even mind the pack on her back. She was too busy thinking about those prospecting tags in her packsack, and the strange trail she had followed, and the smoke she had seen off to the south.

She paused to let Eric and Anna catch up to her. "Did you mark the trail all the way from the mine, Eric?" she asked.

Eric shook his snowy head. "Nope," he said. "I just started doing it when it started to snow."

Anna's heart sank. "How are we going to find our way to the cabin from here, then?"

"We'll just have to be lucky," said Marya. "The storm seems to be letting up a little. I think I can see the trees at the side of the road."

And they were lucky. They almost bumped into the old gray buildings of the Martin Bird mine before they saw them.

As they groped their way around the corner of the old school, they could see a dim light sparkling from a window.

"Look at that!" shouted Eric. "That's the cabin!"

"It's like it's the only light in the whole world," Anna said. She was thinking of the darkness and snow all around them for kilometres and kilometres.

They all trudged wearily up the last slope to the cabin door, unstrapped their snowshoes, and pounded the loose snow from them before leaning them against the log wall.

"Dah-dah-da-dah!" sang out Eric, opening the heavy door. "We're here! What's for supper?"

All three stepped inside. No Toby greeted them. There was no lump on the bed. The covers lay flat and smooth. The cabin was empty!

9

Secrets in the Night

Marya, Eric, and Anna stood breathless, just inside the door of the warm cabin. They had walked so far in the cold, and they had looked forward to this moment of walking into Howie's cabin as if they were coming home. And now there was no Howie Stern!

"Where could he have gone?" Eric said. "He was lying right over there in that bed."

"You don't suppose he went out to look for me — and you two?" asked Marya, in a horrified voice. "Wouldn't it be awful if he were out there and we missed him!"

"He *couldn't* have gone out," Anna exclaimed. "His toe was too sore. It was so sore and swollen that he couldn't get out of bed, even to light his stove!" She just couldn't believe that Howie wasn't in his cabin.

The cabin, small and neat, with everything in its place, looked just as Anna and Eric had left it. The dishes were stacked on the table, and the wood box was still half full with the wood they had split. The fire was still crackling in the stove.

Every corner of the little cabin was warm and cosy.

The three young people stood inside the door, trying to imagine what could have happened to the old man.

Suddenly Anna had an idea. "Here, Toby!" she called softly. "Here, kitty, kitty, kitty."

There was no answering "me-ow!"

"What are you calling the cat for?" Eric asked. "Don't you see it's not here?"

"But Mr. Stern wouldn't take Toby out on a night like this," insisted Anna. "Toby must be here somewhere." She called again, a little louder. "Here, kitty. Here, Toby. Come and have some nice tea!"

Anna tiptoed over and rattled a pan on the stove. "Nice hot tea, kitty. Here, Toby. Come on."

All at once a harsh scraping noise made them all jump!

"Look!" cried Eric. "The bed's moving!"

Sure enough, the old iron bed was rolling slowly towards them. Behind them they saw a light coming from the back wall of the cabin, and heard a cross voice.

"All right, you miserable cat. Go out, then!"

"That's Mr. Stern!" shouted Eric, and made a running dive for the bed. He flopped across it and stuck his fingers into the crack of light that was closing in the back wall.

"Hey, Mr. Stern; it's us! Don't shut that door! Ow! Don't pinch my finger! *Mr. Stern*!"

The crack of light grew larger again. "Is that you, Eric?" asked the old voice. "So you're back?" The crack grew larger still, and Howie Stern popped his head out. "Well, skin it and fry it — I'm glad!" He gave the door a shove. "And if you'd get off my bed, son, I might be able to push this door open."

"Oh, sorry," said Eric and jumped off the bed.

He had been too surprised to move. So had the others. What was Howie doing coming through walls? What was he even doing out of bed?

They stood there with their mouths open as the old iron bed screeched across the floor on squeaky wheels, and a whole section of the log wall behind came with it.

Howie came through the opening with a kerosene lantern in his hand. Then he shoved the bed back, and it just looked like a wall again.

"You see, that's my little secret," the old man grinned. "Everybody thinks this is a one-room cabin. Yep, it sure looks that way — just one little room."

"What have you got back there?" asked Eric. He was burning up with curiosity.

"Well, you see, back in the old days, when there were a lot of people up here looking for gold, it was kind of like the *gold fever* you read about in the books. A man would steal another man's claim as quick as he could think about it."

Toby the cat jumped up on the old man's shoulder, and he patted her with one bony hand as he talked. "It got pretty hard for a prospector to keep his secrets around here. Yes, sir. I knew fellows who would sleep with their maps and their rock samples under their pillows — and that's not very comfortable . . . " Howie Stern chuckled.

"So you built a secret room!" said Eric, his eyes dancing.

"Easy enough to do," said Howie. "Nobody would ever think there was a door in a solid log wall like this." He stroked the smooth, shiny wall with pride. "The bed's attached right to it, so, when I pull the door shut, everything looks right on this side. Nobody ever found out about my room until you folks, tonight! I guess old Toby here let the cat out of the bag."

Howie Stern turned to look at Marya. His sharp old eyes gazed at her thoughtfully.

Marya took off her hood and said, "I'm Marya Savela. I've got your second bottle of pills and some more of your supplies. I'm sorry I couldn't bring all of them. The rest are still with the snowmobile."

"I figured that's who you must be," said Howie, with a straight face. "Wandering around the bush without snowshoes this time of year . . ." He shook his head. "Where were you? And what did you do with your snowmobile?"

Marya gave Howie a brief account of her accident, but she didn't mention "the mysteries."

"Lucky these two young ones found you," said Howie. "Wouldn't want anything to happen to one of Ray Savela's kids. And the rest of the supplies can wait. My pills were the main thing."

Anna noticed that Mr. Stern was wearing a gray wool sock with the front cut out on his sore foot to leave his toes uncovered.

"Your foot looks better," she said shyly.

"I think it was that tea you brewed up for me," Howie said, his eyes twinkling. "It fixed me right up. And I suppose the doctor's medicine might have helped a speck too. Anyway, I sure do feel a lot better. I'll be able to dance a jig by morning! Now, let's see what else your dad put in that supply sack you brought.''

Together they spread out the contents of the sack on the table. Howie hung the kerosene light on a nail above their heads so they could see.

''I think this pack has mostly food in it,'' said Marya, ''— and my survival kit. The packs on the snowmobile have your other supplies.''

When they saw the food spread out like that, all of them realized how hungry they were. Their last full meal had been breakfast, hours and hours ago. And Howie hadn't even had that.

''We could have a stew,'' Marya suggested. ''There's a can of stewing beef here . . . and celery . . . and carrots . . . I could add them.''

''And I've still got a few potatoes around here,'' said Howie. Then his eyes lit up. ''Would you make dumplings too?''

''I'll certainly try,'' laughed Marya. ''It should be fun on the wood stove.''

''We can all help to make the stew,'' Eric said, doing his joy dance around the cabin. ''A great big, luscious, scrumpdelicious stew!''

Eric went outside in the storm to get a pan of snow to melt for water. Anna peeled carrots, and Howie Stern did the potatoes. Marya cooked the vegetables, then popped them in to simmer with the meat. Last of all she made the dumplings.

Soon they were digging into the best meal they had ever tasted.

When they were finished and the plates had been cleared from the table, Marya reached into the side pocket of the packsack under her chair. She drew out the package of prospectors' tags and handed them to Howie Stern. "Dad sent these out for you, too," she said.

The old man plunked the bag of tags down on the table. "Too late for that now," he said. Then he looked up at the three eager faces in the lamplight. "Well, now, it might *not* be exactly too late. Tell me," he said to Marya, "you came around the south end of the beaver pond. Did you see anything ... unusual ... down there?"

Marya's heart jumped. So there *was* a mystery in the bush south of the Martin Bird. All those things she had seen were parts of a puzzle that Howie Stern could explain. Eagerly she started to tell him.

"There was a well-made snowmobile trail through the bush along the old summer road," Marya began.

Eric and Anna were listening with their chins in their hands, their eyes as big as saucers.

"Go on," Howie said. "What else did you see?"

"Smoke!" said Marya. "Off to the south, maybe about a kilometre away. But on my map there's no cabin or *anything* marked down there."

"That's because there *is* no cabin down there," said Howie.

"That's all," said Marya, sorry that she had no more to tell.

"Doesn't matter ... doesn't matter ... ," said the old man thoughtfully. "So that's where they're camped, eh?"

"Who? ... What? ... Where?" shouted Eric, who could keep quiet no longer. "When are you going to tell us what this is all about?"

"Shush, Eric!" Anna said, poking him. "This is serious."

"She's right, Eric," said Howie Stern. He dumped the prospecting tags out on the table. "You see these tags here?" He ran his fingers over the metal shapes. "These are what we nail to the posts when we're staking a mining claim.

"In the old days," he went on, "when you found some gold or silver in the ground, why, you went and got some of these tags and you staked your claim. You measured out your two hectares, and you drove a post in each corner. Then you put these tags on the posts, and that land was yours. All you had to do was register that claim, and nobody else could touch your gold.

"We used to have some fine races, too," he chuckled, "when two fellers would try to stake the same piece of ground. The feller who was the best man in the bush and who could pound in the first post was the one who won.

"But now," he went on, "these fellers come in here with a hundred claims to stake ... "

"What fellers ... what fellers?" Eric shrieked.

"Those fool fellers your sister saw back in the bush," Howie shouted. "They call themselves prospectors! Bah!"

"But what are they looking for?" asked Marya.

"Is it gold?" yelled Eric.

"He sure does get excited," laughed Howie. "Never mind, I get excited about gold myself, son. And when these young fellers come along, calling themselves prospectors, with all their fancy equipment . . . why, I would just love to get in there first and find the ore myself."

"We could help you find it!" said Eric. "We could beat those guys and find it first."

"Well, now, that's what I've just been thinking!" said Howie Stern, his eyes twinkling. "You three seem like pretty good hands in the bush. Let me tell you my problem. You got to see what we're up against."

He stood up stiffly and walked over to the bed. "I guess I'm going to have to take you folks into my back room," he said.

The secret room! Anna felt her breath catch with excitement.

"Bring the lantern," said Howie, "and help me move this bed here."

Marya carried the kerosene lantern. Howie Stern stuck his hunting knife in a crack in the logs that you could hardly see and gave the knife a little twist. The crack grew bigger, and the bed rolled back on its squeaky wheels. The door was open.

10

The Treasure of Strange Lake

It was too dark to see anything in Howie's secret room until he had hung his lantern from a log in the ceiling. Then the others filed in one by one after him.

"Wow!" said Eric. "Look at all the rocks."

The pale-yellow lantern light danced around the little room. From floor to ceiling there were shelves. Every shelf held dozens of chunks of rocks.

"Did all these rocks come from around Strange Lake?" asked Anna.

"Every one," said Howie Stern. "I've been over fifty years collecting the ones you see here from right around this lake."

"Which ones are the gold?" Eric wanted to know.

"Practically all of them have a trace of gold," said the old man, picking up a dull, gray rock and handing it to Eric. "This one here's got a lot of gold in it."

"But it's not even shiny!" exclaimed Eric.

81

"Oh, the shiny stuff — that's *fool's gold*." Howie took a round thing, like a tube with glass in the end, and put it up close to Eric's eye. "Look hard now, in the light," he said. "See those tiny yellow flecks?"

"I see them; I see them," shouted Eric.

"That's gold!" said Howie. "If we cracked it open with my hammer, we'd find a lot more."

"Are the men out there looking for gold too?" Marya asked.

"Those fellers—bah!" Howie Stern said with disgust. "They're looking for nickel."

"You mean like the stuff in nickels?" Anna asked.

"That's right," Howie said. "It's used in lots of other things too. They say there's nickel worth millions of dollars right here under our feet."

"Millions of dollars!" sighed Eric. "But how will they find all that nickel under the snow?"

"That's the point, son; that's the point," said Howie. "They don't need to find it!" He spread out a map of Strange Lake on the table under the light. "They fly over here in an airplane, with some gadget that tells them there's nickel down here. So in they come and buy up all the claims around the whole south end of the lake. You see, they don't need to find the actual nickel — they just buy up all the ground, one hundred — maybe two hundred — claims."

"Then how can we find the real place where the nickel is?" asked Marya, running her finger over the map of Strange Lake.

"With this!" said Howie Stern, holding up a small tube of white powder.

Eric made a grab for it. "What's that?" he cried.

"Easy, son," said Howie. "This is all the Diamethyl Glyoxime I have. We're going to need every grain. I don't want it spilled all over the floor before we can use it."

"Dia-what-sit?" said Eric.

"Never mind the fancy name," Howie Stern said. "It turns nickel ore pink. That's all you need to know." He reached for a piece of ordinary-looking rock on his table. On the bottom of the rock was a bright pink stain.

"Now, all we need to do is find another rock just like it," said Howie, as he pointed to the shelves full of rocks. "If we can find a rock sample that turns bright pink when we wet it and rub this powder on it, we know we've got nickel in that rock. Then, if those fellers haven't beaten us to it, we just stake *one* claim and we've hit the right spot. That's how we old-timers used to work — just one claim at a time."

"But if you find a rock that turns pink, how do you know where it came from?" asked Anna.

"That's a pretty smart question," said Howie, smiling. "Let's get started, and I'll show you how we do it."

"Are we going to test all these rocks? I'll help!" said Eric eagerly.

He scrambled up the step-ladder to the top shelf of rocks and started to bring down an armful.

"Oh, sorry!" he cried, as some of the pieces escaped from his arms and clattered to the floor. "Watch for falling rocks!"

"One at a time, son, one at a time," chuckled Howie Stern. "Just bring them to me one at a time. Then put them back where you got them after we've finished testing."

Carefully Anna took the next sample from Eric's hand and carried it over to Howie. He was perched up on a high stool at the desk. He still had his black tuque on.

"It's a mighty good thing you kids are here to help me," he said, taking the green rock from Anna's hand. "I'm getting kind of old and feeble for climbing around these shelves myself."

He licked his finger and rubbed it on the rock, making a dark, wet spot. Then he sprinkled a tiny bit of the precious white powder on the wet spot and rubbed that in. Anna bent over close to see. Nothing happened. There was no pink stain.

"Nope!" said Howie Stern. "Put it back, and bring the next one."

They soon had a system working. Eric handed a rock to Anna, who took it to Howie for testing. After the test, Marya handed the rock back up to Eric on the step-ladder.

One rock after another was rubbed with the white powder. Many of the rocks had beautiful specks of gold and silver in them that sparkled in the lantern light. Some were smooth and shiny, and some were clear as glass. But none of them turned pink. None of them had nickel in them.

"Got to have lots of patience to be a prospector," said Howie, seeing the weary looks on his helpers' faces after they had finished two whole walls of shelves. "You don't ever give up! That's the most important thing."

"Is that why you stay out here all by yourself?" Anna asked — "because you're still looking?"

"That's right!" said Howie Stern. "I found gold at the Martin Bird more than thirty years ago, and I'll strike it rich with nickel, too — you wait and see. Only this time I'll find enough to make me a millionaire!"

But two hours later they had finished the other rows of shelves. Not one of the rock samples had turned pink. Everyone felt tired and disappointed. It had been a long day.

"Well, I'm going to bed," sighed Howie. "Must be after ten o'clock. If there's nickel around this lake, it must be hiding down a groundhog hole, because I haven't found it!"

"Don't you have any more rock samples?" begged Eric. He was dead tired, but he hated to give up. Howie had said that you should never give up!

"Maybe the old piece I use for holding the door open," said the prospector, "but it can wait till morning. You folks mind sleeping on the floor? I don't usually have overnight company."

They went back out into the main part of the cabin. Eric managed to grab the tube of white powder as he went. He hid it in his jeans pocket.

Howie pushed the bed back to close the door to the secret room. He got a pile of quilts from a cupboard and handed them to Marya. "Think you can make a bed out of that?" he asked.

"We'll be O.K.," Marya smiled. "We'll sleep by the stove with Toby." The big black cat was already curled up in front of the stove, sleeping peacefully.

"Good night, then," said Howie, and climbed into his own bed. Anna noticed that he didn't take off his clothes or his tuque. He just climbed under the covers and seemed to fall asleep instantly.

"Don't blow out the lantern!" begged Eric. "I want to look for that piece of rock he uses to hold the door open!"

"Oh, Eric, he was just kidding," laughed Marya. "There aren't any more rocks around."

"There must be," said Eric. "I want to find the nickel rock."

"You're just crazy," sighed Anna, cuddling down under the quilts. She could hear the storm outside, still beating at the windows. She felt so-o-o-o sleepy.

All of a sudden there was a tremendous crash. Howie Stern sat straight up in bed. The girls looked over to the corner. Eric was sitting on the floor rubbing his head and moaning. The lantern was on the floor beside him.

"What happened?" Marya asked, as she went quickly over to pick up the lantern.

"I noticed a box up there on the shelf and I

thought I could see rocks sticking out of it,'' Eric
said. ''They were rocks, all right. When I pulled
the box down, they fell all over my head.''

''That old box of samples!'' Howie said.
''It's been up there for years.''

Eric reached for one of the rocks on the floor.
Quick as a wink he pulled the white powder out of
his back pocket and tried it on the rock.

''Nope,'' he said, ''no pink.''

He scrambled around the floor finding the rest
of the rocks that had fallen out of the box. ''Let's
try this one . . . and this one . . . and . . . hey!''

Eric leaped to his feet and raced over to Howie's bed. "Mr. Stern, look at this! . . . I found one! I found one!"

All three Savelas crowded around Howie. They looked at the bright pink spot where Eric had rubbed powder on the rock.

"Is that the right color! Is that nickel?" Eric shouted.

"That's it!" Howie beamed. "Bring me some more of that powder and we'll try another spot just to be sure."

"Oh, . . . I think I spilled it," Eric moaned, "but here's some on the floor." Eric scooped up some of the precious powder in his hand and brought it to the old man.

Howie tried another spot on the same rock. Sure enough — it turned bright pink. "Where'd you get this?" he asked.

"From that same box of samples," Eric said. "The rocks went all over when I pulled it down."

"I'd nearly forgotten about those samples," said Howie. "Haven't ever tested them for nickel. Now, let's see if there's a number anywhere."

"A number?" asked all three Savelas.

"Yup! That's my code. See, here it is — No. 203 — right here." Howie showed them the funny, old-fashioned numbers, written right on the rock. "Now you kids all turn around and hide your eyes."

They did. They could hear the prospector squeaking around in his bed.

"You can turn around now," he said finally.

When they turned around, they saw that Howie had a long, thin, black notebook in his hands. He had found it somewhere in his bed.

"Another secret hiding place," thought Anna.

Howie turned the pages quickly. "Here we are," he said, "number 203. That's the number on the rock sample. Can you read what it says there? My eyes aren't too good for this small writing." He handed Marya the book. Eric and Anna looked over her shoulders.

There were rows of numbers on one side of the page, then a row of dates, then a row of places. It looked like this:

No. 201   May 15, 1954   South Arm
                         Near mouth of Beaver Creek
No. 202   May 23, 1954   Same as No. 201
No. 203   May 27, 1954   South Arm
                         Rock outcropping
                         one kilometre east
                         above shoreline

Marya read it out loud.

"That's the place, then. Yup, I sort of remember that big outcropping of rock. Sticks out like the front of a ship. It was more than twenty years ago I picked up that piece."

"Can we go tomorrow?" Eric begged.

"Well, those prospector fellers work fast. If your sister saw them up on Clarabelle Ridge, there's not much chance we can beat them," Howie Stern said. "But we can get up real early in the morning and try."

11

The Race Begins

By seven o'clock the next morning, Howie Stern and the Savela children were snowshoeing along the trail to Clarabelle Ridge. Howie went first, then came Anna, then Marya. Behind them came Eric, flopping along on his snowshoes.

Howie had been right about the medicine. His toe was still a little sore, but the swelling had gone down. Now he could get his socks and boots on.

The snow had stopped some time in the night. Every tree they passed was wearing a big, fuzzy snow hat. Even the tiny twigs were piled high with snow. As the sun rose in the sky, the trail was bathed in a pink glow.

Eric started singing. "Oh my dar-ling, oh my DAR-ling . . . "

"Shhh," said Howie Stern. "We don't want them to hear us coming. There's the smoke from their fire. They'll be just over that hill."

"Look, there's the camp," said Marya.

The snowshoers stood on the top of the ridge and looked down. The prospectors' tents were right below them.

"Look at their snowmobiles," Anna said. She pointed to two big, double-track machines covered in canvas and a deep pile of snow.

"They'll go like rockets!" said Marya, and Anna could tell she was really excited.

The prospectors' camp had four tents, set up in a circle. Each tent had a stove pipe coming out the top, and logs around the bottom to make a low wall. As Howie Stern and the children watched, the door of one of the tents opened. A man came out, looked up at the sky, and stretched.

"City feller," muttered Howie Stern. "Just getting up at this hour. Bah!"

"It's a good thing he has his back to us or he could see us easily," said Eric.

"Just keep still, Eric, or he'll hear you, too!" warned Howie.

"They're getting ready to go staking," the prospector continued. He pointed to the man who was uncovering the snowmobile and shaking the snow off the canvas covers. "We'd better make tracks."

They slid quietly back down the top of the ridge.

"Where do we go now?" asked Eric.

"We'll head for the South Arm of Strange Lake," said Howie. "I know a shortcut from here. We'll see if they've been staking in that direction."

"What do we look for?" asked Anna.

"Keep your eyes peeled for a tree stump cut off about as high as your head," said Howie. "It'll have the top squared like a block, with those shiny metal tags you saw nailed on each side."

They trudged off through the snow, each of them hoping that the men from the city would be going in the other direction that morning. If they could only reach the place where Howie Stern had found the pink rock before the strangers did!

They had only gone a short distance before Eric gave a shout. "I see one — there's one of the claim posts!" He dashed off towards it, almost tripping over his snowshoes. The others followed.

Howie brushed the snow off the top of the birch stump. "Yup," he said. "Look here — this is their number-one post." He showed them how the prospectors had written their name and the date and time they had staked a claim.

Anna read: 13 February 1978, 2:00 p.m. "Does that mean the city prospectors have beaten us?" she asked.

"Can't say till we get to the South Arm," answered Howie, "but they're working in that direction, that's sure."

He sounded worried.

"Well, c'mon," cried Eric, charging off on his snowshoes. "We've got to get there first!"

"That youngster reminds me of a young moose!" chuckled Howie, as he watched Eric — "always off on a wild rampage somewhere.

"Over this way," he called to Eric. "You're headed the wrong way, son."

"Do you always know the way to go?" Anna asked, following the old man's steady footsteps. He seemed to walk slowly, but she found that she could hardly keep up to him.

"This bush is like my back yard," Howie said. "I've been poking at the rocks and watching the trees grow around here for more than fifty years.

"Look there!" he added suddenly, pointing to some big tracks that crossed their trail. "That's my friend the lynx!"

"Friend?" said Marya in surprise, coming up behind them to look at the tracks.

"Well, I don't *really* know him personally," chuckled Howie. "I used to try to trap this big old feller, but he's too smart for me. I've seen him once, just at sundown, and he runs circles around my cabin all the time — just to show he's not scared of me."

"Do you know where he lives?" asked Marya.

"Not for sure," said Howie, stroking his chin, "but I have an idea it's somewhere on that high land down at the end of the beaver pond."

"Then it's *our* lynx!" said Anna, feeling very excited.

"What lynx?" cried Eric, who had finally caught up with them.

Anna pointed to the tracks.

"That's the fierce animal that almost ate my sister!" said Eric. "The one that lives in that smelly cave."

Then they had to explain to Howie Stern how Anna had almost walked into a lynx in a snowstorm, and how Marya had stayed dry and warm in its cave.

"You're a lucky young lady to see a lynx so close up," said Howie. "They hunt at night, and they're mighty shy."

"Lucky lynx," sang Eric, "lead us to the nickel — nickel."

They marched on, with Eric singing his silly lynx songs behind them.

In a few more minutes they had reached the shore of Strange Lake.

"There it is," said Howie, pointing across the lake. "That's the big outcrop that looks like a ship — see her there?"

At the same moment, Marya's sharp ears heard a sudden noise in the wilderness quiet.

"Shush!" she said.

They all listened. Far away, they heard the buzz of a snowmobile. As they stood there quietly, the sound became louder and closer.

"Sounds like our friends," said Howie, pulling the tuque off his ear to hear better. "Dang those fellers. I hoped they'd dawdle over breakfast a little longer than that! Well, we don't want them to see us here, or they'll hurry even faster. Come

on, folks. We're going down a hole like a family of foxes."

He led the way to a snow-covered mound of rock. Marya, Eric, and Anna quickly dug out a place behind the rock for them to hide. Just in time they crouched down behind the rock. The big yellow machine came growling over the hill only a few hundred metres from their snowshoe trail.

"Look at the machine break trail!" said Marya in admiration. The prospectors' big snow machine wasn't having any trouble with the deep snow drifts as it chugged down the slope towards the lake.

The big machine purred as it hit the smooth snow and shot off across the ice at top speed. It left a sharp, clean trail across the lake and disappeared into the thick trees on the other side.

"No slush," said Eric. "Too bad. They must be going over seventy kilometres an hour."

"We're going to have to work mighty fast to stake out claims on that bluff before they get there," said Howie, shaking his head as they set off once more on their snowshoes.

"On that big machine, they can go a lot faster than we can," said Anna, hurrying to keep up.

"Faster," said Howie, "but noisier too. That machine makes lots of noise. We're going to know where those fellers are all the time, and they don't even know we're here."

They reached the ice on the lake and started across. For once, Eric didn't sing or whoop or shout. "I'm a mighty hunter," he thought, "on the track of a huge polar bear. I can't make a *sound*!"

Finally they reached the other side, and now they had a steep climb ahead of them. Howie chose a trail that seemed to go straight up the side of the outcrop of rock. He had to stop often and rest, leaning one hand on his bent knee.

The others struggled up behind him. It was not easy climbing in snowshoes. Eric had a terrible time with his. Twice Anna's slid out from underneath her and she fell.

"Just watch how Howie does it," said Marya. "See, he takes his time and makes sure one foot is secure before he lifts the other one."

Anna watched and got the idea. Eric did the best he could in his clumsy boots.

Carefully, step by step, they climbed the steep bluff. They were all panting and out of breath when they reached the top.

Howie was a few paces ahead when they reached the edge of the trees. He stopped and stared. Then he tore off his black tuque, threw it on the snow, and stomped on it with his snowshoes.

"Blast the fladerrap!" the children heard him cry. "The city fellers have staked her!"

"*What*?" shouted Eric, forgetting that he was a silent hunter.

"They've staked the whole danged thing. That's their claim post right over there!"

12

Eric Tries to Stand Still

Howie Stern sat in the snow with his tuque in his hands, staring at the prospectors' claim post.

"We were beat," he said. "Fair and square, we were beat."

The others stood around him, feeling very disappointed. Not far off they could hear the rumble of the prospectors' snowmobiles, as they hurried through the bush, staking still more claims.

"It doesn't seem fair, though," Eric said, and Anna and Marya knew how he felt. Howie had been living in this part of the country all his life. He knew every rock and tree. The two prospectors from the city didn't know the country. Some instrument in an airplane told them there was nickel down here, so they were buying up all the land. It didn't seem fair at all!

Anna snowshoed over to look at the claim post. It was a birch tree, cut off about 120 centimetres from the ground. The top had been slashed with an axe on four sides to make a square.

Eric came over to join Anna. "Sure is too bad," he said. "Mr. Stern won't even be able to look for gold any more because these guys will own the land."

Anna ran her fingers over the shiny, gold-colored tags. "These look really new, don't they?" she said.

"Brand new," agreed Eric. "I bet they just did this yesterday."

Eric was examining all the sides of the post. "Hey!" he shouted excitedly. "There isn't any tag on this side. Maybe they just got this far before the snowstorm and had to quit!"

"What does that mean?" asked Anna.

"I don't know," said Eric. "Let's find out.

"Mr. Stern," he cried breathlessly, running over to Howie, "what does it mean when there's only tags on three sides of the post and no tag on the other side?"

"What? Slow down, son. I didn't catch most of that."

"When there's tags on three sides," said Eric again, waving his hands around to show what he meant, "but the other side is bare."

"Are you sure?" asked the old man, getting stiffly to his feet.

"Sure I'm sure — I'm sure, aren't I, Anna?"

"Come and see, Mr. Stern," called Anna.

Howie Stern snowshoed over to them. He walked all around the post and looked at the tags. There was a gleam in his eye as he ran his hand over the smooth white wood of the bare side.

"What does it mean?" asked Anna, bursting with curiosity.

"Well, now, ... " said the prospector. "Well, now, this is very interesting!" His eyes were twinkling. He looked at the post, and then he turned and looked at the big outcropping of rock below them. He put his hand up to his nose and shut one eye and squinted down his hand.

"I'd say this post about cuts the rock in half, wouldn't you?" asked Howie.

Eric stumbled over and stood in the same place and put his hand up to his nose the same way. "Yup, just about in half," he said, although he had no idea what he was doing.

"What are you looking at?" asked Marya, coming over to see what it was all about.

Howie broke a stick and traced a circle in the snow. Then he drew a cross in the circle like this:

"Here's our post," he said.

"It looks to me like our young fellers quit before they finished here. They staked one, two, three claims from this post, but they didn't stake number four."

"You mean half the rock isn't claimed?" asked Marya.

"Looks that way," chuckled Howie. "Wouldn't it give those fellers fits if we were to stake the other half!"

"And this is where the nickel is!" whooped Eric.

"Then would half of the mine belong to you?" asked Anna.

"That's the idea," said Howie. "Now we got to get our North East post first . . . "

"Whoopee!" shouted Eric. "We're going to make a stake!"

"I think you'd better hurry," said Marya, who had been listening to the snowmobile engine off in the bush. "It sound as if the prospectors are headed this way."

"We're going to stake so fast, lightning couldn't catch us," said Eric.

"What do we do first?" asked Anna.

"Help me get this packsack off and find my axe and compass," said Howie.

"I'll help," said Marya quickly.

"Good. Now I want you two to take this compass and keep the needle pointing on north." He showed Eric and Anna how to walk and watch the compass needle. "And I want you to count exactly 660 steps. Think you can do that?"

"Can we do it!" said Eric. "Of course we can do it."

Anna nodded too.

"And you and I, young lady," Howie said to Marya, "will mark blazes on the trees with the axe. That'll show our staking line nice and plain." He laughed. "I want those fellers to know for sure that this land has been staked right out from under their noses." He handed his axe to Marya, then turned to Anna and Eric.

"Now, when you kids have counted 660 steps straight north, you stop. Got that? You stop dead, and don't you move from that spot until this young lady and I catch up to you."

"I'll be a post," said Eric. "I'll stand so still you'll be able to pin tags on me and leave me out here till spring."

"Maybe *I'd* better be the post," giggled Anna, laughing at the idea of her brother ever standing still that long.

"You better get going," said Howie Stern. "This time we want to beat *them* fair and square."

Eric and Anna set off. Anna counted their steps. "One . . . two . . . three . . . four. Watch it, Eric," she called. "Your steps are too big."

"I'm trying to watch this dumb needle," Eric complained. "It keeps jumping all over the place!"

"Maybe I'd better hold the compass," suggested Anna. "You're wobbling a lot, you know, Eric."

It was true. Eric found it hard to walk in a straight line at any time. It was just natural for him to dash and run and wiggle and jump everywhere he went. Now, in snowshoes and boots that didn't fit, he couldn't walk in a straight line no matter *how* hard he tried.

"I am *not* wobbling!" he shouted. "It's this darn needle." Then he realized they shouldn't be fighting. This was too important a job.

"All right, Anna," he said. "You give it a try."

Anna took the compass and got the red needle to point to the letter "N." Then she tried to walk very slowly and carefully until she could do it without making the needle jump. "O.K. !" she called back to Eric. "I've got it. Start counting."

Marya and Howie were behind them, marking slashes on the trees with the axe.

Eric and Anna were still finding it hard to count and walk straight north as they stumbled over rocks and fallen trees.

"Three hundred and forty-two, three hundred and forty-four — I've never counted up so high in my life," thought Anna.

They were both trying so hard not to lose track of their counting that they didn't hear the

104

sound of someone else moving through the bush close by. They didn't notice the crisp, sharp sound of the axe marking trees, or, if they did, they thought it was Howie and Marya coming behind them.

Finally they had gone far enough. "Six-hundred and sixty . . . Whew!" Anna said. "I didn't think it would be so far!"

Eric came up quietly behind her. "Stop! " he said, in relief. "This is it!" He was almost whispering in the silent woods.

They were in the middle of a thick jack-pine forest. Anna had to bend and break the lowest branches of the trees around her just to make room to stand like a post on the spot.

It was very quiet. Suddenly there was the sharp "thunk" of an axe hitting a tree.

"That's not Howie Stern," Anna thought. "That sound came from ahead of us!" She bent over and peered through the thick pine branches. She could just make out the flash of something bright red as another "thunk" echoed through the bush.

"What is it?" whispered Eric, seeing the frightened look on her face.

Putting her finger on her lips, Anna pointed through the thick trees.

"It's the prospectors!" Eric moaned in an agonized whisper. "We've got to hide . . . "

"We can't!" Anna whispered back. "We're a post, remember? Howie Stern said not to move!"

13

Howie Stern's Contraption

"If that man keeps coming this way," Eric thought, "he's going to walk right into us. I wish I could turn myself into a *real* post right now!"

Anna was wishing hard that Marya and Howie would take a long time to catch up to them. If only there were some way to tell them. "If I could turn into a crow," she thought, "I'd fly around calling *CAW — CAW*. Then they would know there was danger."

But Anna and Eric couldn't turn themselves into anything else. All they could do was stay crouched down, close to the snow. The heavy tangle of jack-pine branches hid them from the prospector, but he was very close. When he broke a twig, it seemed to snap right in their ears. One or two more strides and he would be on top of them!

Suddenly, a louder sound made them clutch each other tightly. The big, grumbly snowmobile was bringing the other prospector up the hill.

"What if the snowmobile crunches right into the bush!" thought Anna in dismay. "We'll *have* to move then."

The big machine roared to a stop just millimetres from them. They could see the yellow helmet and big, black goggles of the driver as he walked over to join the other man.

"Just about finished here?" the driver asked.

Eric and Anna held their breath, not daring to move.

"I guess so," said the first man. "My last stake should be somewhere in the middle of that pine tree."

"*Our* pine tree," thought Eric in panic.

"Oh, you don't have to be that careful!" said the man in the helmet. "Just whack off this poplar here and call it quits."

"Right," said the first man. "It's close enough."

"Whew!" thought Anna. "It's close enough, all right!"

They heard the axe biting into a slim poplar, and the creak of the tree as it started to fall. It was so close that Anna put her hand over her mouth to keep from crying out.

In a minute, Eric and Anna heard the quick tap of the hammer as the men nailed the tags in place. Then there was a roar from the snowmobile engine as it started up.

"I'm not sorry to be finished up here!" the first man shouted to the other. "I had a creepy feeling all the time that there was someone watching me."

"Evil spirits," laughed the other. Soon the sound of the engine drowned out their voices as the machine sped away.

"Evil spirits!" roared Eric, when the snowmobile was safely away. He rolled on the ground with laughter. "That's a good one. My sister, the evil spirit . . . "

"My brother, the idiot," said Anna. She didn't feel like laughing yet. That had been too close for comfort.

When Howie and Marya caught up to them, Anna was still shaking. Eric told the story, adding lots of danger and excitement.

"You did real well," said Howie. "Won't those fellers be surprised when they come back and find our posts!" he added gleefully. "What do you say we cut down this prickly old pine right here — since it's already been so useful."

Within seconds, Howie Stern's skilful hands had cut and slashed the tree. The tag was pinned to one side, along with this message, written with a timber marking pencil:

15 February 1978
10:00 a.m.
Howie Stern
Licence B. 1000

"Skin it and fry it," said the old man, "that sure makes me feel good!" The others admired their post standing so straight and sturdy there in the bush.

By 10:30 a.m. the other three posts had been cut and marked with the tags.

"Well, that's that!" said Howie.

"Boy, I'd sure like to see the faces of those men when they see that post," said Eric. "We did it, didn't we, Mr. Stern? We staked the claim."

"All except the hard part," answered the prospector.

Anna, Marya, and Eric stared at him in astonishment.

"What hard part?" asked Anna, not believing her ears.

"Well, now we've got to get back to town and *record* that claim before these other fellers do," said Howie. He was quickly packing his tools in his sack. "Let's go!"

"Back to town! What's he talking about, Marya?" Eric asked, as they scrambled after Howie.

"I'm not sure," said Marya, "but if we have to go into town, we've got a problem! It's a long walk."

"Is Dad's snowmobile broken?" Anna asked, slipping and sliding down the steep hill.

"I sure hope not," Marya sighed, "but we don't have the strength to dig it out and get it up on the trail."

After that, the three didn't talk because they were too busy trying to keep up to Howie. He seemed to fly across the lake and vanish into the trees as if he had rockets on his snowshoes.

"Have you noticed," panted Eric, "that Mr. Stern seems to be just slumping along, and yet he's really flying?"

The prospector was waiting impatiently for them at the cabin when they stumbled up to the door, red-faced and tired out.

"Thought you were never going to get here," he said crossly. "Those fellers are going to be down here in that fancy machine of theirs as soon as they see my name on that post. We have to beat them into town."

"We'll never beat that machine on snowshoes!" exclaimed Eric.

"Did I say we were going to *walk*?" asked the old man. "No, sir; I think it's time I took my contraption into town. Come and help me get it out of the barn."

"What next?" wondered Anna, as they trudged after Howie down the old deserted street of Martin Bird.

They stopped at an old shed. It leaned at a crazy angle, but the snowdrifts had been cleared away from the doors.

"This is my other secret," said Howie Stern. "You've heard about my famous limousine?"

"The car the Queen rode in?" gasped Anna, her eyes growing as large as saucers.

"That's the one," chuckled Howie, swinging back the doors. "And there she is."

The morning sun shone into the dusty shed.

"There's no car there!" said Eric in a disappointed voice. "Just a lot of old pipes, and a steering wheel, and, . . . " he stopped, speechless.

"Yup, I sure have stripped it down," laughed Howie. "Just wait a second here, while I crank it up."

"Does that thing go?" asked Eric.

"Just listen!" said the old man. He gave a handle at the front of the contraption a mighty heave. There was a loud explosion from the back. Howie cranked again, and a tremendous roar filled the air.

"There it goes!" cried the prospector, and climbed up on a seat that seemed to be hanging in mid-air. "Watch out; we're coming out the door," he shouted, and the three children jumped back out of the way.

"LOOK at that!" Marya exclaimed in wonder, as the contraption appeared. "He's turned the Queen's limousine into a bush buggy!"

It was the strangest-looking machine they had ever seen.

"He's got airplane skis on the front . . . "
said Eric.

" . . . and two snowmobile tracks where the
back wheels should be," said Marya.

"But where's the limousine?" cried Anna,
disappointed. She had expected to see a long,
shiny, black car, with big, soft, padded seats,
covered in velvet.

"Climb aboard!" called Howie. He grinned
at Anna's disappointed face. "Look here," he
said, helping her climb up. "I saved the crown,

just in case some little girl might get to worrying that it wasn't the Queen's limousine at all." There, above the steering wheel, Anna saw a tiny silver emblem in the shape of a crown.

"I use the contraption to haul wood and such like," explained the prospector. "Never thought I'd be driving it back to town. Hold on; here we go!"

There was only one seat, like a tractor seat, for Howie Stern. Eric, Marya, and Anna stood on the platform and held on to the curved pipes to keep from falling off. The contraption bumped over the snow on its airplane skis. The snow-mobile tracks in the back drove it forward down the street.

"It really works!" shouted Marya.

"I still don't understand why we have to go to town," yelled Eric above the engine noise. "What's so important?"

"Well, it might be that two people think they staked the same mighty important claim at the same time," Howie Stern explained. "Then it's who gets to the recording office first and registers that claim that has the best right to it."

"You mean our claim isn't really ours until we get it written down in a book in town?" Anna asked, trying to understand.

"You mean those other prospectors might say they staked our claim before we did?" Eric said, suddenly understanding.

"I think we're going to find out," said Marya, "because here they come!"

14

A Race to the Finish

Marya had been watching the trail behind them, when, all at once, the prospectors' yellow snowmobile had appeared out of the bush. It slowed down at Howie's cabin, and one of the men jumped off.

Meanwhile, the driver noticed the old man's contraption disappearing down the road. He rubbed his goggles in disbelief. Then he shouted to the other man and pointed. "There he goes... "

The other man raced back to the snowmobile and jumped aboard.

"Hey, stop! We want to talk to you!" they called out to Howie. The yellow snowmobile shot forward to follow the contraption.

"Guess they saw our posts!" chuckled the old man.

"Will they catch us?" Anna asked. She was holding on as tightly as she could.

"Maybe, maybe not," said the prospector, pointing the contraption up the hill.

"Come on, do your stuff!" shouted Eric, pounding on the frame.

"Watch out, Eric; you'll fall off," said Marya, putting out a hand to steady her reckless brother.

The contraption lost speed on the long hill. When they reached the top and looked down over the beaver pond, the yellow machine was close behind. The men were still shouting.

"Stop, Mr. Stern. We want to talk to you."

"I bet you want to talk," said the old man. He glanced behind and saw that the snowmobile was rapidly catching up.

"Did you say there was slush on the beaver pond yesterday?" he asked the children.

"Some near the shore," Marya said quickly.

"Should be more today. We're going to try something fancy. Hold on tight, now!"

Howie gunned the contraption straight down the hill. The yellow snowmobile was just a shadow away. At the very last second, the old man gave a wild whoop and turned his steering wheel hard. The contraption almost turned over. It rounded the corner on one ski and sped away down the shore of the beaver pond.

The prospectors' machine wasn't so lucky. Snowmobiles are hard to turn suddenly. It shot out onto the ice, and then sank right into sixty centimetres of icy, sticky slush!

"Oh, boy! I know how that feels!" whooped Eric. "They'll never get out of there!"

"That should hold them for a while," Howie agreed.

"Will they be all right?" Anna worried.

"Oh, we'll come back and give them a hand ... after we pay a visit to the recording office," Howie promised.

In no time at all they had reached the bridge at the end of the pond and were on the smooth, hard trail back to town. The Queen's limousine just flew, now that it didn't have to churn through heavy drifts.

Howie was concentrating on driving his noisy contraption. So were the children. They cheered Howie on. They "pushed" to help the contraption up Miner's Mountain. They were all concentrating so hard that none of them noticed another noise. The roar was getting louder and louder behind them.

It wasn't until they were at the top of Miner's Mountain, looking down at the town of Strange Lake, that they looked back.

"It's the prospectors again!" howled Eric.

The big yellow snowmobile was almost halfway up the hill and coming fast. In another moment it would be on top of them.

"Blast the fladerrap!" said Howie. "They must have got themselves out of the slush and come across the beaver pond!"

"Can we beat them?" Anna cried.

"We can try!" shouted the old man. "Hang on, kids. It's going to be a wild ride."

"We'll never make it," thought Marya. "They're too close now."

Howie put his old contraption into gear, and away they plunged down the hill. Anna shut her eyes and held on for dear life. When the car hit a big bump, the three young people were pitched in all directions, but somehow they managed to grip the steel pipes and not get thrown off.

"Whoo-ee! That was a good one," shouted Howie. "You kids O.K.? Good! I'm going to really let her rip now!"

Howie Stern took his foot off the brake and let the car go.

Faster and faster the contraption flew down Miner's Mountain, bouncing and rattling. The wind howled in the children's ears, and the cold air stung their cheeks.

As they rocketed down the hill, they picked up more speed. They raced across the flat at the bottom, hit the snowbank, and flew 300 centimetres into the air before landing with a terrific bump on the road.

"Where's the city fellers now?" shouted Howie, not daring to take his eyes off the road.

"Right behind us!" answered Eric.

"Is the Mining Recorder's Office still on Main Street?" Howie Stern shouted back.

"Same place," Marya replied. "But it closes at one o'clock on Saturday."

"Come on, then, one more burst," cried Howie, and stamped on the gas.

People on the streets of Strange Lake jumped back in alarm as Howie's contraption roared through town.

Right behind it came a powerful yellow snowmobile.

Howie Stern was perched high on the seat of his contraption. Eric had his legs and arms wrapped tightly around one of the pipes. Marya, in her blue suit, was standing up. Anna was clinging so hard to her pipe support that her hands ached.

Outside the Mining Recorder's Office the contraption screeched to a stop. Its four occupants crowded in the door just ahead of the two prospectors.

Mrs. MacDuff, who worked in the office, looked up in alarm at all the noise. Then her eyes widened in astonishment and pleasure as she recognized Howie.

"Howie Stern!" she cried. "Well, it certainly is good to see you in here ... after all these years!"

"I'm here to record a claim, Mrs. MacDuff,"
said Howie quickly.

"Well, are you really? Isn't that nice . . . "
Then, for the first time, Mrs. MacDuff seemed to
see the young people and the two strange men.

"We're recording claims too," said the driver
of the yellow snowmobile. "We represent the
Consolidated Nickel Company and we have a cou-
ple of hundred claims in this area."

He got no further.

Mrs. MacDuff held up her hand. "You'll
have to take a seat," she said in a firm voice.
"Mr. Stern was first."

"Hurrah! Wowee!" shouted Eric. "We're
first; we made it!"

"Eric Savela," said Mrs. MacDuff, *"you'll* have to go outside in the cold if you can't behave yourself."

"That's right, Eric," said Howie. His eyes had a special sparkle. "Mrs. MacDuff was recording clerk here back in the days of the first Strange Lake gold rush. She always sees that things get done properly."

All three Savela children leaned their elbows on the counter while Howie filled out his forms.

"Did these three Savela children help you in staking your claim?" Mrs. MacDuff asked.

"Help me! Well, I just guess *so.* I couldn't have done it without them," said Howie.

Eric turned to grin wickedly at the two prospectors, who sat grimly waiting on the hard-backed chairs.

"We're going to have a lot of explaining to do at head office," said one of the men.

"Well, that's that," beamed Mrs. MacDuff. "All recorded and legal. It's your turn now," she said to the prospectors.

As they stood up to record their claims, one of the men came over to Howie. "My employer will be in touch with you," he said.

"No doubt he will," chuckled Howie. "No doubt at all."

15
Adventure's End

It was almost one o'clock when they left the Mining Recorder's Office.

On their way to the Savelas', Howie made one more stop. "Have to see a geologist friend of mine," he said. "He lives near you and works for a mining company around here." Howie reached into his pocket. "Just happened to bring this rock sample from our claim along with me. Think Frank Hill might test it for me, even though it *is* Saturday afternoon."

Before Howie had parked his contraption, the geologist was rushing out of his house, putting on his parka as he came. "Well, Howie Stern," he exclaimed, "what a surprise! Couldn't believe my eyes when I saw that contraption drive up to the door."

"Glad to see you, Frank," said Howie, grinning. "My assistants and I have come to ask a favor. Maybe you already know these three Savela young ones?"

"Not by name," said Mr. Hill, "but I certainly know who they are, and I know their dad. Glad to meet each of you. Now, tell me, what have you four been up to?"

Howie and the children told him, as quickly as possible. Then Howie brought out the rock sample and asked Mr. Hill about testing it.

"I'll go down to the mine lab right now," said the geologist. "I'm almost as excited about this assay as you are. Where can I call you about the results?"

"We'll be at our place, Mr. Hill," said Marya. "You could call Howie there."

Back home, Eric and Anna lay stretched out on the living-room rug.

Sitting in the big, comfortable, purple chair was Howie Stern, with a mug of hot tea in his hand.

Marya came in from the kitchen with mugs of hot chocolate for Anna and Eric. "Watch you don't spill it on the carpet," she said.

"Back to civilization," said Eric. "Every time people give me anything to eat they tell me not to spill it on the carpet. I liked it better back at Mr. Stern's place, where there wasn't any carpet."

Anna thought that she would never move, it was so good to lie there and rest.

Just then the back door banged open, and they heard their dad come into the kitchen. In another moment, Mr. Savela stood in the living-room doorway, leaning on his cane. He looked worried.

Marya stiffened, getting ready to face her father with the news about his snowmobile.

"There's the craziest-looking piece of

machinery I ever saw sitting out in front of this house," Mr. Savela said, "and a bunch of kids climbing all over it . . . "

"That's how we got here," shouted Eric, jumping up from the rug. "That's Mr. Stern's contraption. You should have seen us racing the prospectors to the mining office and beating them, and staking our claim!"

"Claim? Prospectors? What in thunderation are you talking about?"

Mr. Savela looked at Howie Stern, sitting there grinning in the armchair. "When I heard they'd brought you into town, Howie, I figured your foot must be in bad shape — that maybe you needed a doctor. What's all this about racing — and where are my sled and my snowmobile?" Mr. Savela turned to ask Marya the question she had been waiting for.

"Well, Dad, the sled's back at the beaver pond," she said slowly, "and the snowmobile..."

"Why did you leave it there?" her father interrupted.

"Slush!" shouted Eric. "You should have seen the slush, Dad. Ninety centimetres thick."

"Hush, Eric," Marya said. "But Eric's right about the slush, Dad. I had to go around the pond and break trail," she explained. "Then my ski snagged a branch, and the snowmobile rolled over the bank. I'm *awfully* sorry it happened, Dad, but it happened so fast . . . and I just couldn't get the snowmobile back up the hill by myself. And then the kids came to find me, and we found some nickel ore in Mr. Stern's cabin with a date and a place on it, and this morning we staked the claim . . . "

"Stop!" Her father held up his hand and sank onto the couch. "I think I'd better sit down for the rest of this."

Eric raced over with a cushion. "Here, Dad," he said, "lean on this!"

In no time at all, the whole town of Strange Lake was in an uproar. Everyone had heard about the nickel ore being found on the shore of the South Arm. And they'd heard about how Howie Stern and the Savelas had beaten the prospectors from the city. The men had been seen heading back to pack up their gear at the bush camp.

Everyone seemed to know that Howie and the Savelas were waiting for the geologist's report on the nickel ore. The town was holding its breath. If the ore was good, it might mean a new mine and a new life for many people in Strange Lake.

Meanwhile, some of the neighbors organized a search party to go and tow the Savela snowmobile back to town, with the rest of Howie's supplies.

"Better pick up Howie Stern's cat at the Martin Bird," Mr. Savela said to the men, "and bring in some of Howie's clothes. I think he'll stay with us for a few days."

Late in the afternoon, Eric and Anna were showing the other children in town over, around, and through Howie Stern's contraption.

124

"It used to be the Queen's car, you know," Anna said, showing them the crown.

"Stripped down for action — she can turn on a dime!" Eric added, describing how they'd led the prospectors down into the slush.

Marya came to the door. "Hey kids!" she called. "It's the geologist calling Howie. Come on in!"

Anna and Eric raced for the door. As they kicked off their boots in the porch, they could hear Howie Stern on the phone.

"Well, thanks, Frank. That was mighty nice of you to do the assay on a Saturday afternoon. I know it's not one of your regular working days."

There was a long, long wait while Howie listened and didn't say anything. Then a big grin started in the corner of his mouth and began to spread. The grin travelled up his face until his eyes started to sparkle and his hand came up to tear off his tuque.

"Well, say . . . ," Howie chuckled. "That's good news, Frank. Yup, I guess they'll all be pleased to hear it. Thanks again."

He hung up the phone and saw Marya, Eric, and Anna waiting with their mouths open.

Howie Stern rubbed the scruff of hair on top of his head. The grin was so big now that his face looked as if someone had turned a light on inside it.

"Are we millionaires?" yelled Eric, who could never wait for news.

"Not yet, son, not yet," Howie Stern chuckled, "but you never know. The sample from that claim we staked is rich, all right. Frank says it's the best he's seen in years. And to think that rock sample was sitting up there in my cupboard for twenty years! Just think of that!"

"Ya-*zoo*!" shouted Eric, dancing around the kitchen. "Dad, did you hear? Howie Stern's ore is *really rich*! It's going to be a gold mine . . . a nickel mine, I mean!"

"I've been thinking I should move into town if I'm going to have all this mine business to take care of," Howie Stern continued. "Anyway, Ray, those Friday trips of yours must be a fool nuisance sometimes."

"You're welcome to stay with us till you find a good place," said Mr. Savela.

"Oh, boy!" cheered Eric. "Howie Stern *and* Toby *and* Howie Stern's contraption! Things are going to be *really* interesting around this house."

"The only thing that worries me is leaving my cabin with no one to look after it all winter," said the prospector.

. "We'll look after it," put in Marya quickly. "The kids and I will go out every weekend and make sure everything is all right."

Suddenly they heard the sound of snowmobile engines. The neighbors were back.

Marya rushed to open the door — and a black cat flew past her.

"Hi, there, Toby," laughed Howie. "How've you been?"

"How is Dad's snowmobile?" Marya asked anxiously. "Is it O.K.?"

"One ski is bent a little," replied one of the neighbors, "but that seems to be all. Your dad can look at it in the morning."

"Oh, Dad, I'm sorry about the ski," said Marya. "Your brand new machine!"

"Never mind, girl," said her father. "A snowmobile can be fixed. It's just a lucky thing you weren't hurt!"

"Yes, never mind, Marya," agreed Eric. "Howie Stern's new mine will pay for a dozen snowmobiles. We're going to have a mine, a really big one, with deep, deep tunnels . . .

"Hey!" Eric added suddenly, "I never told you how I fell down a mine shaft out there. Boy, I was almost killed!"

Everybody laughed. Then they all listened to Eric's story.